Luis de Miranda

WHO KILLED THE POET?

Translated by Tina Kover

THIS IS A SNUGGLY BOOK

WHO KILLED THE POET?

> *"I hope all will be well."*
> Ophelia
> —Shakespeare, *Hamlet*

Prologue

More passionately than usual

In his Ville-d'Avray studio my brother stared at the child, who had squatted down on his haunches. It was just after ten o'clock in the morning on April 20th, 2010. *I'm hallucinating*, thought Bardo. *If I try to touch this kid's hair, my hand will go right through him.* He took a step forward and put out his hand. Slowly.

> *I wish I were at the bottom of a well*
> *or in some far-flung country.*
> *I would close my eyes*
> *and find my world turned to dust.*

The spirit-boy looked up. Bardo touched his hair and the little skull beneath, which had a thick, watery consistency, like jelly. When he pulled his hand back, it was dry. My brother let out a strangled sob, choking it off halfway through when someone knocked on the kitchen door.

The visitor held a package, his face half-hidden by a hood. When Bardo went to open the door the child kept close to him, slipping his hand into my brother's. A strange sensation, like touching the untouchable.

The coffee-capsule deliveryman pushed back his hood but said nothing to the little being; it didn't seem that he could see him. Bardo hesitated, searching for a plausible explanation. "This is my son," he finally ventured to the man in the doorway.

The deliveryman looked at the empty space beside Bardo. He saw that my brother's fingers were tensed and curled, as if holding an imaginary hand. This wasn't the first eccentric customer he'd dealt with. A little solicitude, he had learned, didn't hurt.

"He looks like his dad. Sign here."

Bardo let go of the little hand to scrawl his name, struggling to conceal his consternation beneath an air of dignity. He took the package of coffee capsules, said goodbye, closed the door, and turned to Bernardo.

"What do you want?"

Without answering, the child looked at a photo propped up next to some books in the kitchen library. He stared at the face of a young woman of twenty or so, her gray-blue eyes shadowed by dark circles, her skin pale, hair dyed a deep shade of red. In this six-year-old image, Ophelia and Bardo were holding hands, joy visible in their faces.

"She was pretty," he said in a clear voice, his lips barely seeming to move. "Do you still love her?"

"I don't know. We haven't seen each other in a long time. I don't know what she's up to now; I only hear from her once or twice a year."

"Why?"

"It was . . . complicated. She lives in Hamburg now, I think."

"Do you want to see her again?"

"I don't know."

I knew the whole story of Bardo and Ophelia, down to the smallest twist and turn, because my brother always told me everything. I was his confidant—but not his keeper, and despite the doubts I'd had at the time about the part-French, part-English girl's character, I hadn't felt like it was my place to judge their relationship, which had, after all, made my brother so happy it was like he'd sprouted wings. Wax ones, maybe . . .

Ophelia had been for Bardo what they call a fatal passion. The kind of passion that engulfs everything, sometimes turning it sublime and musical, sometimes heavy and smothering. When he thought about her now he pictured himself clinging to the side of a cliff on the very edge of Europe, dangling fifteen or twenty meters over the void.

It had been in Portugal, almost six years earlier, in July. They'd known each other for three months. Ophelia had said she had a serious illness—leukaemia. She was only twenty, and to hear her talk, it might be her last summer. Bardo was enchanted by her rebellious allure, her unpredictable personality; by her Byronesque accent and her presence, which managed to be intense and diffident at the same time. By her clever wildness and her thighs. She listened to a lot of music, often classical, especially Rachmaninov's piano concertos (gut-wrenching and snobbish) and what she referred to, with a smile (she never really laughed), as "bad goth rock": groups that played dark, macabre stuff, like Emilie Autumn and Calabrese and Diary of Dreams. She collected vampire films. When he was with her, my brother felt like better things were on the way.

That summer they'd found themselves on the Sintra coast between Cabo da Roca, the westernmost point in Europe, and Praia das Maçãs. They'd spotted a stretch of beach accessible only by a steep cliffside, which awakened Ophelia's thirst for both verticality and danger. What had she been through in the past, to make extreme situations her natural element?

My brother had always suffered from vertigo, while she was as supple as a vine and as reckless as a fiend. The descent took long minutes on a path that grew more and more narrow, until they were inching along a ledge no more than ten centimeters wide, their bodies pressed against the rockface, high above the earth below (horrifyingly high, as far as my brother was concerned, but no distance at all in the eyes of the initiator).

Bardo fought to stay calm. He knew that if he looked down he might fall, compelled to drop off into the void. They had no idea if the path they were following was even negotiable. Maybe they should turn back, which would almost mean rock-climbing barehanded. Ophelia, who was outpacing him quite easily for a leukaemia patient, alternated between making fun of him and pausing to encourage him softly until he caught up with her. Bardo would have never taken a risk like this if he hadn't thought she was ill; no, he believed her cancer story completely, even though the climb had a certain metaphorical quality, like a cry for help. And he didn't want to lose face in front of her.

Since the beginning of their relationship he'd vacillated between compassion and admiration for her. He'd yearned for exuberance for a long time, and from the time of their first meeting at the foot of the Arc de

Triomphe he'd sensed a kind of elegant turbulence in her. Hers was the sublime and tormented beauty of a cathedral. But her insouciance was clearly just a pose; something was eating away at her. The knight in Bardo rose up. He would live up to the highest expectations and save her from the dragon.

One day, maybe a month before the episode on the cliffside, she had called him at his office and asked if he had a dressing gown, and if he wanted to meet her for a dive into the fountain at the Place de la Concorde. He'd made some excuse to his fellow architects and hurried out. The couple had enjoyed a "sacred" swim in the gilded fountain and then strolled around La Madeleine church in their too-short white robes, giggling maniacally at the shocked glances of tourists. During his relationship with Ophelia, my brother's colleagues criticized him for slacking off at work; rumors swirled that he was going out with a girl who was kind of crazy, and that she was the one pulling his strings.

On that summer day on the edge of Europe, they had eventually reached the beach safe and sound. It was an inlet, surrounded by craggy rocks. The waves seemed indifferent to Bardo's feat, but Ophelia had realized just how much he loved her. She started to regret her lies, but she'd gone too far to recant them. That night, they made love even more passionately than usual.

1

I will change the past

The world is spinning. I'm adrift. I've tried to anchor myself to the ground in the Fausses-Reposes forest. But the more still I am, the more my senses whirl and the words echo in my head: *Bardo is dead.* The summer solstice is only just past.

He was the poet, whereas I don't think I'm much of a writer at all. All I have are a bunch of disparate impressions outlining the empty place where he was. Nausea. The endless longing for him. I spread my arms wide, drawing in a deep breath. My pleasure in being alive seems to have run dry. Is that possible? *I'm only one man,* I cry out. I want to strip grief bare of lyricism in what I'm about to write. It's cooler here, under the branches. I'm in the woods where my twin brother liked to walk, just above the Ville-d'Avray cemetery. *Bardo.* It's more than a name; it's a collection of images, a haunting noun. And a crime as yet unpunished. But not for much longer.

I close my eyes. The scents of the trees rise up around me like memories of shared intoxication. I could do with a bit of light-headedness right now; a cool breeze drifting through my brain like the veins in a leaf. Something to give me just a little relief. The time to tell it, to untangle it. To feel something other than suffocation, the weight of the past, creeping up on me.

The ferns radiate an otherworldly light. *The luminous floral dimension*, he wrote in his last notebook, twenty-three days before his death.

Death. Such a stupid word . . . 'Bardo' was his pen name. He was born Bernardo, and he died at the age of thirty-eight on Saturday, May 15th, 2010, in Hamburg. Someone pushed him . . .

Pushed. Shoved. Bumped into. Caused to fall off the platform at the Sternschanze metro station. *Sternschanze*: it means, I believe, 'starry overlook' in German. I'm sure in twenty years that will make me smile, but right now I can only manage a grimace. But I'm discovering the true power of words.

I'm a wounded man, but you won't hear me complain too much, because this is war, and this story is a battle.

The police found a little wooden kaleidoscope in his pocket, gift-wrapped. I've kept it as evidence, and one day I'll jam it down the killer's throat. Because there is a killer out there; make no mistake. And if he speaks a human language I'll shut his mouth for good.

The criminal was—according to the few eyewitnesses—a young supporter of the English Fulham football club. I'd love for the whole thing to turn out to be a nightmare. The guy was drunk, let's say, and he accidentally jostled my brother just as the train was pulling in, and then ran off. Everything seemed to happen so *fast*, Officer! Three days later, on May 18th, I found a postcard in my mailbox from the Kunsthalle museum in Hamburg, showing a mask by Fernand Khnopff dating from 1897: an angelic face surrounded by foliage, with a wing over each ear. On the back of the card, my brother's handwriting. Lines composed, apparently, the night before he died:

> *One can continue to grow up*
> *At the top of an overcome drop,*
> *To beguile the future*
> *We will change the past.*
> *Your Passiophile*

I was so bewildered I stopped crying. That message from the beyond soothed me in the devastated days leading up to the funeral. Bardo, who sent me postcards from everywhere (including Paris), had developed the habit of signing them as "Passiophile". He'd explained the neologism on one of the cards once: some creatures lose their will to live and wither away the moment they stop feeling passionate about something. My brother was naturally optimistic, but he tended to lose himself sometimes in that dark place that has been trying for years to crush us, to grind us up, to toss us under the wheels of machinery and protocol: that place of panic that he called "Objective Relative Opulent Reality" (OROR). Bardo was sometimes reckless, too curious, too furious (by OROR's standards), but he was far from crazy. If he wrote to me that we could change the past, then it must in some way be true. But how? That's what I have to discover.

Here's my answer to your last note, Bardo:

Drop?
Collaborative act or confidential crime?
Stronger than us: abandon, benefaction?
Ascent . . .

Your Avenger

The burial took place fifty meters from Bardo's home, on the edge of the Fausses-Reposes woods, in the Ville-d'Avray cemetery, at dawn on Tuesday, May 25th, 2010. Shortly afterward I moved into his garden-level studio close to the tombstones. Among others, this marble alphabet includes the grave of Boris Vian—an echo from our teenage reading, from the books that taught us to cherish waking dreams. Bardo is hanging out with Boris now, and everyone else is probably listening to their conversations. My brother used to say that the still of the evening, among these giant trees, this army of shadows, was like a border between the urban world, hard as stone, and the world of the forest; a tiny, vital shift. Sometimes a doe even ventures near the ancient wall encircling the cemetery.

No one prepared me for this. I used to feel as light and carefree as a deer myself. I've never truly experienced solitude before. Sometimes I just stand here, among the trees. I've spent two months weeping, but sometimes I feel an unexplainable surge of joy. An impression, a memory, an element of Bardo in the air . . .

After the funeral our parents, dazed and inconsolable, stayed for a week in my Paris apartment. I terminated the lease a couple of weeks ago; I'm living in his world now. They've gone back to Portugal, where—until Bardo's death—they'd been enjoying

15

what you might call a quiet retirement. They call me every day, their voices slow and halting. I'm their last link with a past that made sense. In order to comfort them I steel myself, and I will do the same to conduct my investigation.

I've spent two months wandering in the place where, surrounded by greenery, Bardo passed hours calling forth the energies that make up life. Sometimes I'm ashamed of the sour words I've written. He knew how to say things in a different way. His handwritten notebooks are proof of that, and maybe his death is, too—because people who say or do things differently cause nightmares for those who simply accept the status quo.

Hints of chlorophyll mingle with the scents of my brother in the little apartment. His notebooks, his clothes, his white furniture, his books, his wrought-iron bed, his silence, and more notebooks, filled with his writing, more books overflowing the two bookcases, one in the bedroom and one in the kitchen. The garden twice as big as the apartment itself, tucked away in this English-style house with its old-fashioned bricks and the Virginia creeper vines climbing the walls. The high desk, turned to face the window, where in the mornings, before going to earn his living in a Parisian architectural firm, he stood and worked on his poems. I'm writing this book, this investigation report, at that same tall black lectern. I'm standing too, drawing on all my strength in this world haunted by my twin brother's presence, weak but driven to keep going. Am I hunting one murderer, or more?

A poet has died under suspicious circumstances. I hope this disappearance can serve as a warning. I

16

want anyone who wonders what this event has to do with them to revisit those moments of purity they have experienced just after a dream, or a coincidence, or a caress. When they've had a wild hope come to pass, or been amazed by the mysteries of the universe around them. When they've had a pipe dream or heard faint voices. I want people who think—but won't say—that poetry is just needlepoint for eunuchs, to listen to the whispers of their mind, the drumbeat of their desires, the sighs of their boredom. To stop suppressing their rebellion against the toad-croaks of ugliness and un-healthy comfort.

Who killed the poet? *Careful.* I have to keep a cool head, no matter how impossible that seems. Other-wise, who knows—someone might shut me up, too.

I'm going to take apart the mechanism of the facts, piece by piece. And, if I can, I will change the past.

2

People say a lot of things

The Hamburg police are apparently either completely useless or extremely slow, and the surveillance cameras don't show the moment of the accident except for indistinct shapes—a sort of drunken adolescent lunging forward, his face half-covered by a scarf, running into Bardo sideways and causing him to lose his balance, before running away. And no "foolham" FC supporter has turned himself in. So, I'll conduct this investigation by myself. I'm sure the reader will figure out some things before I do; I'm writing these words half-blinded by confused emotions that are hard to put down on paper, especially for someone who's never been any good at crafting the monstrous or the invisible.

Pragmatic thinkers will wonder what Bardo was doing in Hamburg—a city which, he remarked to me before he left, has been the cradle of modern capitalism since the late sixteenth century. And why he, who hated the vapid inanity of football, chose to go there during the Europa League final. That, as it happens, was just a coincidence; he'd taken advantage of the Ascension bank holiday to go looking for Ophelia.

I'd always been suspicious of Ophelia Lovelace, with her name and personality like some character in a Gothic romance. She was my brother's former flame, a devil-may-care sylph he was still quietly in love with despite their breakup five years earlier. She'd already come very close to killing him on a cliffside once (sorry, Bardo, if I'm being too hard on her).

If he was murdered, isn't she a party to it, more or less? The police found her mobile telephone number and address in my brother's wallet—a fact of which I was made aware by a neurasthenic fifty-something police inspector called Kreiss, who barely attempted to speak English and gave me that particular piece of information as if getting rid of something embarrassing.

Ophelia claimed to be descended from Ada Lovelace, Lord Byron's daughter. I'd always had my doubts about the authenticity of that genealogy, especially in light of the other lies she told, but Bardo—who had eventually met her father—seemed to believe that she was telling the truth on that matter at least.

When I went to Hamburg on Sunday, May 16th to visit the morgue of the Eppendorf hospital and 'identify the body'—it was intact and beautiful, my brother having 'only' been clipped by the train—I was too upset to think about Ophelia. I called her when I got back to Paris, and when I told her I needed to see her she hung up on me with what sounded like a sob. She hasn't returned any of my calls since.

I returned to Hamburg on the following Friday, four days before the funeral, hoping to find an explanation—and maybe to bring Ophelia back with me so she could attend the ceremony. When I went to her address on Vereinstrasse, north of the Schanze quarter, I spent three hours staring at a closed door. I rang some of her neighbors' doorbells, but the building remained deaf and mute. In the end I mentally told Ophelia to go to hell—if she wasn't already there.

I went back to Inspector Kreiss's office, but had no luck there either. Even now, more than two months later, the police haven't been able to identify the criminal. They just keep repeating to me that the person who caused the accident was alone, of average height, and apparently young and broad-shouldered; that he seemed drunk and wore sunglasses, a baseball cap, and, according to witnesses, a scarf with the arms of the Fulham football club, which had just been defeated in the final against Madrid.

Why wasn't Ophelia with my brother at the Sternschanze station when the accident happened? The gift-wrapped kaleidoscope, which I examine every day as if it might be a clue—was it for her? From what he'd told me about his trip, Bardo was supposed to have had dinner with her on Thursday, May 13th, two days before the accident. They hadn't seen each other for five years and had kept in touch only sporadically.

He'd wanted to see her in order to try and solve a mystery. Another mystery, which might very well be related to his ante-mortem postcard. I have to talk about it, even though it might call my brother's mental health into question. Or maybe my own.

Since April 20th, my brother had been having conversations with a child only he could see.

A spirit-child who said his name was Bernardo, just like my brother, and who seemed fascinated by his relationship with Ophelia.

Was he a manifestation of Bardo's soul? Or was my brother in the early stages of some kind of psychosis in the last weeks of his life? No, that kind of simplistic explanation isn't worthy of him. Maybe my way of telling things isn't worthy of him either. I feel clumsy, like ideas are buzzing in my veins, and I think I'm going to need a lot of self-control to convey the complexity of this story. I'm sorry, Bardo; I'm fumbling in the dark. I write two sentences and collapse on your bed exhausted; then I get back up and force out a few more inadequate words, with feelings jolting through me like electric shocks.

In the midst of all my confusion, an idea has started to emerge: find Ophelia Lovelace, wherever she is — because according to the police, she's left Hamburg.

Not wanting to push, I didn't call you on that Friday the 14th, the day when you must have sent me your last postcard; I wanted to wait for you to bring up the subject of Ophelia, when you were ready. We were supposed to have dinner on Sunday the 16th, a few hours after your return to Paris. I'm sure you would have had strange things to tell me, as usual. Your life story was a poem.

They say that when you meet your double, it means you're going to die soon. They say a lot of things.

3

Since you woke up

At midnight on April 20th, 2010, twenty-five days before the accident, I met my brother at the Sir Winston, an Anglo-Indian-themed pub located near the Arc de Triomphe—a monument I'd never given a second thought until six months earlier, when it played an important part in Bardo and Ophelia's romance. The pub's Chesterfield sofas and fine woodwork evoked a cozy bygone era that had long since been embalmed and archived and transformed into a ghostly reflection. My brother stood at the bar, looking pale and uneasy, but still with that beautiful air of innocence that was his trademark—or, rather, his pen-name. Physically, some people had remarked recently that we no longer looked as identical as before; lifestyle and character affect the face as much as a night of dreams—or nightmares.

"Don't you see him?" Bardo's voice was anxious. He gestured at something next to him. I responded in a low murmur so as not to draw any attention.

"The little boy?"

"He says his name is Bernardo! Tell me I'm not crazy!"

"I could, but I wouldn't be a very good brother if I did."

He threw me a distraught look. I ordered a couple of lemonades to cool our heads and refresh our spirits and then, because people were looking at us, I steered him toward a table at the very back of the pub.

"You could never be crazy, Bardo," I said, wanting to reassure him. "Even if you tried. It's probably just a mental breakdown. Or maybe a syndromic manifestation of your desire to procreate."

He still wouldn't smile. The server set two yellow drinks on the table. I decided to dial back the humor. "So, he's right here with us?"

My brother frowned. "He's watching you. When I touch him it feels like watery jelly. He listens to what I say and sometimes he talks back."

With a slight grimace of distaste, I stretched out my hand toward the place my twin had just indicated. I couldn't feel anything. I was starting to worry now. Being eight minutes older, I'd always played the role of big brother.

"Bardo. Stay calm, and tell me everything that's happened since you woke up."

4

Before he became Bardo

It's Saturday, July 24th, 2010, and I'm in a room at the Hotel Shakespeare in Vilnius, Lithuania. The weather outside is sluggishly hot. I've barely left my room (the Venice room, it's called). I'd better rejoin the present with this story.

What am I doing in Lithuania? I'm looking for Ophelia Lovelace, relying on my own intuition and a few deductions. Let's get back to the spirit-boy.

My brother worked on his poetry at home almost every morning, unless he was walking in the forest; for him, the two activities were complementary. On that day he was standing at his desk as usual, both hands resting on the wooden surface, facing the window that overlooked the garden. He closed his eyes, as he often did to find inspiration or draw energy from the great wellspring of Life. Then he wrote:

> *Why do we sing*
> *When everywhere generosity*
> *Lies sleeping?*
> *To stimulate the velocity*
> *Of thread and throne ascending.*

Out of nowhere, a vision came to him.

He saw himself as a child, running joyfully through a green field. The sun shone warmly and the little Bernardo's feet were cushioned by the soft grass. The vision-boy had familiar features; long black hair that curled at the ends, and a handsome Latin face with dark, laughing eyes: my brother at the age of four or five. Almost no one could tell us apart.

On the right side of the field a massive tree rose up, its leaves and branches sweeping almost to the ground. The child went to the tree and stroked its trunk.

The bark was rough but pleasant to the touch. He looked into the palm of his hand and murmured the single word *life*, as if christening what he saw there. Then he walked slowly around the trunk, examining it. There was a vertical slit in the bark, like an eye turned on its side; an area where the wood was lighter and smoother, as if the trunk, wanting to be naked, had tried to slip out of its sheath.

A sudden noise shattered the image, an anonymous helicopter skimming the undersides of the clouds above Ville-d'Avray. Reality, attempting to reassert itself.

Bardo opened his eyes and looked around—then jumped, stifling a cry. The child was there, standing quite close to him and looking perfectly real.

My brother rubbed his eyes and—in an attempt to pull himself together, or maybe out of fear—kept them closed. Sun to shadow, shadow to sun. But the vision had followed him inside his head.

The child was surrounded by an urban landscape now, in a city that looked like Berlin. It was night, and Alexanderplatz was framed in neon red, yellow, and blue lights. Tram tracks ran alongside glass-fronted buildings. The whole area looked anemic, like most of Europe's commercial thoroughfares. To the child's left stood a large cinema. He went to the right, toward a restaurant, though he was neither hungry nor thirsty. Behind him, there was a sound like the beating of wings. He turned around.

A huge white bird rose into the sky. The child jumped, wanting to go with it. He felt as if he, too, could fly.

He hovered just above the ground at first, but then rose up a few hundred meters, into the sky above the city. Amid the clouds surrounding him he discovered rows and rows of books, like an enormous aerial library. When he looked down, he saw that his feet had come to rest on a wooden floor of the same color as the slit on the tree in the field.

The child squatted down. He was drawn to the books, but he sensed that if he continued to move, this place would disappear too. And with that thought alone, the floor gave way and the books vanished in drifts of smoke.

The little boy now found himself on an ancient battlefield. The ground around him was littered with corpses, and pikes and swords jutted out of the dirt. Warriors fought and screamed oaths. Some of them were bearded and some were clean-shaven, and none of them really knew what they were fighting for—which only increased their fury. The child stood still amidst the carnage. He could hear the hissing of arrows in flight, like tiny drills. A horse collapsed at his feet in gravity-defying slow motion. A cloud of dust billowed up.

Everything vanished again, into the wind. Then, silence.

The child breathed in and out, in the middle of nowhere. He was not quite five years old, but he felt as if he had lived a great deal, as if he had spent long periods on earth, and his body had grown old and then young again. He understood joy and expectation, desire and betrayal, slavery and freedom. All these feelings seemed intertwined. There was something illusory in their persistence: reality exploded in shards if you fixed your gaze firmly on it.

Bardo mustered the courage to open his eyes.

He knew, even without looking away from the window, that the spirit-child was there, just to his right.

Probably, he told himself, the apparition was just a part of his own soul. My brother, as he fought his own private battles, was sometimes as rough as tree-bark; sometimes as innocent as a child. Outside, the leaves of the rosebushes sparkled in the sunlight like so many tiny mirrors. Bardo turned his head. The child wore jeans and a blue polo shirt. His clothes, like his face, had a strange luminosity. He looked back at my brother, his face serious but without hostility.

There was something like an urgent question in his eyes.

Bardo's panic had gone. The child standing there so quietly, so calmly, no more than a meter away, didn't seem to be the manifestation of an unhealthy thought, or the harbinger of some tragedy. My brother met his gaze for a few seconds, and then asked simply:

"What's your name?"

"Bernardo. Like you," answered the child in a clear voice.

Bardo hesitated for another beat. Then, humbly: "Are you my soul?"

The child didn't answer; he seemed to be pondering the question. He moved silently around the studio, his attention drawn to a book lying on the kitchen table. Bardo had begun a book at breakfast that morning: Hermann Broch's *The Sleepwalkers*, set in Berlin. But I also remember that he'd spent a winter evening in Alexanderplatz a few years earlier, shortly after his breakup with Ophelia. He had found it a desolate place, he'd told me then, "like a hologram created by solitude."

The child was two meters away from Bardo now, on the doorstep of the room, terribly alive. My brother shivered, took a step back. Pulled a photo album from the bookcase. A slightly yellowed photograph was stuck between two pages near the beginning of the album.

I'm holding that photo in my hand right now. It was taken by our parents, thirty-three years ago. There he is, standing in a grassy field in the sunshine, next to a tree. The spitting image of the apparition.

Bernardo, before he became Bardo.

5

An explanation for everything

You might think it's strange, the way I'm beginning and ending each chapter, as if I were the director of a dramatic film, blurring things as much as the smoke I can see billowing from an industrial chimney stack out the window of my new hotel. But without this method I'd be like rainwater, seeping into every crack so I don't evaporate.

It's July 25th, 2010. I've left Vilnius, that city of cheerful disrepair and medieval shadows, where the trees and the baroque churches seem to be fighting against the future. I took a bus that wound through dozens of kilometers of woods and fields and dumped me out yesterday on the edge of the Baltic Sea, in the ghost city of Klaipeda. I'm writing this in a room near the port with an uneasy sense of imminent danger. Tomorrow I'm going to take the ferry and then travel down the Courland Isthmus, a narrow strip of sand dunes between two seas, to the town of Nida, where I hope to find the red-headed siren.

The heatwave of the past few days has given way to a cool freshness that is more in character for north-eastern Europe, which seems to be floating in a sort of bubble of its own, detached from modern history. My reasons for looking here for Ophelia probably seem pretty weak on the surface: last July 13th she told the Hamburg police that she was leaving the country for a month, and took a flight to Vilnius. I found out that she and her companion (because she's not travelling alone) spent two nights at the Hotel Shakespeare (an obvious conclusion once I'd looked at the list of fifty or so hotels in the small city). She asked the reception desk there to book her a hotel room in Nida.

Instinct tells me that she's still here. In a (perhaps overly) trusting moment, I've just sent her a text telling her where I am and asking her to wait for me. Will she answer, or take the opportunity to run away again?

My mind is filled with doubts, especially now that I've found out the age of her travelling companion. It's a child.

Last night, I wandered the deserted streets of Klaipeda. A saxophone-player did his best to ruin the atmosphere of the Germanic old town. I had a beer at the Hemingway Pub, the name recently bestowed on an old wood-paneled bar that claims to have served dinner to Hitler in 1939 and now plays commercial crap on an endless loop: Shakira, Lady Gaga, Madonna, and other similar succubi whose artistic horizons begin and end with the letter A. And I thought about the sign I'd received in Vilnius, the one that told me I was on the right track.

It was late and I'd gotten lost among the winding streets, in the labyrinth of my own Middle Age. On an old wall, not far from Klaipeda Street and the Reformatai Park, I suddenly came upon this bit of graffiti, representing the number 888.

Shakespeare and the eight hundred and eighty-eight breaths: the great discovery that had come out of Bardo and Ophelia's romance. I should tell you about that. It might help to explain the spirit-boy's power.

But first, let's jump backward in time and space again, to the Sir Winston pub on the night of April 20-21, 2010, twenty-five days before my brother's death. As he talked, I started to wonder if maybe he *was* going a little bit crazy, in spite of everything:

"Bardo, I'm starting to wonder if maybe you *are* going a little bit crazy."

He was anxious. I felt like I shouldn't have joked about it. What is insanity? Isn't the worst kind of madness what Bardo himself called "self-sabotage"—that all-too-common disruption of grace by uncontrollable urges? Bardo's last handwritten notebook, which I've kept with me along with some of his other writings, includes these lines:

> *Beautiful madness, aware of the world around it, will make suggestions which, given free rein, will come to the surface and unravel in excesses too healthy for their time, like a bet made by a non-rational universe.*
>
> *A dangerous game, that will be won some-day by more than one person and be the ruin of society. Life plays endlessly on our desires.*
>
> *I see humans as arenas from which will emerge—defying censures and stays, rising up against self-sabotage—certain attractors, strange angels who, by the power of their endurance, hostile to the principle of reality, will create folds in time.*

The dream of the slave is that no one will be free. He tells himself, rather, that some people will be like black holes of generosity, absorbing time and space to slow pain down at the source, and regurgitate shackles as blossoming possibility.

On April 21st, in the Sir Winston pub, around two o'clock in the morning, I put down my lemonade and say soothingly to Bardo, looking him straight in the eye:

"You can't let this worry you too much. There's an explanation for everything."

6

The good things in life never last very long

The spirit-boy was still staring at the photo, as if trying to figure out Ophelia's personality. Then he looked at my brother with determination.

"Did you really love her?"

"More than anyone, at the time. It lasted a year. She was my lover, my friend, my enemy, my sister. I've never felt so strongly that a woman needed to be the mother of my children. It was like some deep, primal instinct. But she didn't love me back enough, and she was only twenty. Sometimes instinct can be wrong."

The child gave a brief smile and quietly put the photo down. He walked to the glass kitchen door and looked out at the sun-washed garden. A ray of light caught his body and illuminated it with supernatural intensity. Without turning around, he murmured:

"Can I go out in the garden?"

Bardo watched as the child seemed to melt through the closed door and reappear outside. He stared after him for a long moment and then, dazed, went to take a long shower.

"And he was still there when you came out?" I asked in the dimly-lit Sir Winston, even though I already knew the answer.

Bardo nodded. "When I got in my car to drive to the office, he was sitting in the passenger seat."

No one in the architectural firm where my brother spent his weekday afternoons had noticed the spirit-boy. Bardo was the only one who could see him walking silently around the office, curious and jelly-like. My brother had a hard time concentrating on his work; once he saw a colleague walk right through the child's body, pausing only for a split-second, as if she had felt a draught.

That evening, while I was having a carefree conversation with a near-stranger on the terrace of a café in Le Marais, Bardo found himself in a Saint-Germain bar with a couple of his acquaintances whom he'd bumped into while wandering the streets trying to understand what was happening to him. The child watched them eat, invisible to the eyes of everyone but my twin. At around eleven o'clock the Bernardos (large and small) left Paris and headed back to Ville-d'Avray. But Bardo only made it as far as Sèvres when, just before midnight, he decided to turn back and call me.

It was April in Paris. The sun intensified our desires and melted the icicles in our minds. My body was craving pleasant surprises, and a long winter as a singleton had left me feeling both deprived and ready for anything. I was so light-hearted, only four months ago! Happier than most people, even, because I was lucky enough always to have someone there who never disappointed me, who was never dull or stupid or inconsistent. Now—now that I'm in this world alone—there's nothing around me but shifting gazes and ethereal presences. Who can I count on? I hate even to write this, but sometimes I'm in so much pain that I feel like I'm being physically wounded. My parents are afraid that I might do something drastic, but they're only making me feel worse by calling me every day. Sometimes I wish I could just stop breathing. Bardo's postcard is the only thing that's kept me going so far; the belief that his death must have some meaning, a meaning that depends partly on me.

Why did I think Ophelia would wait for me in Nida? She probably took off with that kid the minute she read my text. Our buses might even have crossed paths without us seeing each other, here on this little bit of sand and forest between two seas.

Discouraged, I leave my bags in a room in one of Nida's blue-and-white wooden hotels and go for a walk on the beach. I sit down on the white sand, my back against a large dead branch. Isn't there any way to bring Bardo back? Memories wash over me.

I'm back on the evening of April 20th at around eleven o'clock, shortly before my brother's anxious phone call, in the winding streets of Le Marais—an ancient part of town that has managed to resist destruction by geometric city-planning but not purification by museum, and is crammed with private mansions we'll never live in. I was on the terrace of the Café des Philosophes on the rue Vieille-du-Temple, gazing warmly into the shifty blue eyes of the lovely Annabelle, whom I'd just met, an uncertain feminine presence whose desirability I was still assessing.

I doubted that we'd end up in bed together; there was something dark and morose about her, despite the surface harmony of her features. She asked me if I had friends, if I liked Lisbon, if I was a Don Juan. I let out a long laugh—the last one for a long time, as it turned out—and looked at her face; it was like an overgrown child's, lovely and morbid, framed by raven hair.

"What's the difference between Don Juan and Casanova?" I asked, answering her question with a question.

She pretended to be interested in my riddle, but I could see that she didn't really care about the answer, that her spirit was too anxious about everything and nothing. Undaunted, I pressed on:

"Casanova was *military*. Don Juan was *mille e tre*."

Annabelle smiled absently. "I think I've never been in love, you know," she said.

Now this is an interesting woman, I said to myself, even though she's a bit too evanescent.

She spent her days drawing agonised airborne images of herself. Her face was serious and sincere as she spoke to me from behind her third glass of Sancerre:

"I think about death a lot. All the time, really. When you create something, it means you want to kill someone."

There is, amid the dregs of Paris's artistic community, a kind of morbid aftertaste that rings fatally false—along with a healthy dose of convivial alcoholism (extremely common among Westerners between adolescence and death). I find the ease with which young Parisians get drunk disgusting, myself; like Bardo, I rarely drink or smoke, preferring the sting of a glass of tart lemonade to any drug. Paris is a cacophonous cradle of Miracles; its denizens are sometimes sleek and sometimes monstrous, but always strange. Bardo loved to make up portmanteau words, and I could hear him murmuring in my ear:

"Our civilization really must be rebuilt around something other than universal *hormony* . . ."

He actually used to wish for a mutation, a pagan redivinisation of the human species. He often talked about how we needed to renew our connection to the "vital *infranimal*" or "infrational" lifeblood. Usually I could intuitively understand what he meant. But I've never had his steadfastness of character, his almost hypnotic spiritual fixedness; I've often shifted from one state of consciousness to another at the first sign of adversity, like a rootless plant or a child jumping from game to game.

The Baltic Sea has brought back my last innocent memories. To flesh out the bones of my conversation with Annabelle a bit, I'll tell you that I picked up the menu lying on our table at the Café des Philosophes and asked her if she wanted to have dinner. No, she said, wrinkling her nose; it made her uncomfortable to chew food in front of people she didn't know.

"You'll probably think I'm anorexic, but I just think eating in front of other people . . . it's the last taboo that isn't taboo."

I sort of knew what she meant; at any rate, her uniqueness amused me. But I also told myself that this girl was too unhealthy and too much of a snob to bother with. An awkward silence descended upon the terrace of the Café des Philosophes.

"There are three fundamental truths," I said abruptly to her, taking on the air of a fox-terrier behind my glass of Perrier. "The first one is that Life is pure pleasure."

She thought about that for a moment. "Wait, are you saying that my unhappiness is just a figment of my imagination? God, I hate it when people try to minimise how I'm suffering! Could you possibly be any more arrogant?"

"I'm not talking about you specifically," I said, carefully keeping my voice level. "I mean LIFE, the flow of vital energy, the Great Creative Becoming. Don't tell me the two of you have never been introduced?"

"Oh," she said, childishly thoughtful. "Yes, I mean, when I play the piano or draw . . ."

"There are several ways of keeping yourself as close to Life as possible. One of them, according to Shakespeare, is to look someone in the eyes for as long as it takes to draw eight hundred and eighty-eight breaths."

"That seems like it would take a long time."

"It does. Almost an hour."

"What does it mean, though?"

"It's the secret my brother discovered six years ago, while he was on a crazy adventure with a red-headed princess."

"Really? Do tell!"

"Later. First, the second truth: an individual human consciousness can only copulate with Life through concentrating and being open at every second. Order and vitality are dialectically connected, and that's the third truth: humans need to have a single focus, otherwise they'll just sink into a state of lethargic chaos."

"So we're never fully alive?"

"Exactly. All we can do is get as close as we can to the fabric of immanence, to the vital maximum. Otherwise we go crazy. Our consciousness becomes scattered, fragmented."

"Or we sink into a trance. Or we're dead."

"In other words, ultra-alive."

"Do you think the fabric of immanence runs underneath the terrace of the Café des Philosophes?"

I smiled. I liked talking fashion with her.

I inhaled deeply. Annabelle suddenly seemed magnificent. What had started out as just the umpteenth variation on the Parisian theme of flirtation on the Philosophes terrace *might* just be turning into a romantic encounter . . .

I looked at Annabelle, trying to capture her gaze. Her mind seemed elsewhere already, but I wanted to bring her back. It was April 20th, 2010, just before midnight. My phone vibrated.

It was Bardo, in a panic. The good things in life never last very long.

7

To see her again?

Is there something in the air that pushes you to give up? I've decided to stay on the Courland Isthmus for a few days, in Nida, here amidst the silence of the dunes and these ancient woods that were pagan for so long, one of the last places in Europe to be converted to Christianity. There's nothing to do here except go for long walks, and think, and remember. What if Ophelia ran away just to protect me? I may be descending into a nightmare, but there's nothing that says I have to run down the stairs.

I can't think where she could have gone. Is she leaving Lithuania? I send her another text: "I won't give up on the truth."

My brother and I might have shared the same uterus, but sometimes we behaved as differently as a shooting star and an earthquake, a blackbird and a mockingbird, a muse and a satyr. Our mother saw him as the romantic and me as the easygoing one, a dichotomy she knew was exaggerated but which suited her taste for putting things into neat categories. It's true that Bardo tended to get himself into tricky situations when he was in love—especially where

Ophelia was concerned—while I've always been more cautious.

Sometimes I think fate is determined to deny me any kind of lasting happiness where love is concerned. I'm probably too sceptical, too much of a misanthrope perhaps, which is why I always admired Bardo so much for his ability to be so passionate about another human being. Sometimes he seemed weighed down by a kind of melancholy, a vague feeling of guilt, and maybe a premonition of death, but at least he got a taste of the deeper things in life, whereas I still feel much too hung up on surface images. Often, when confronted with an up-close manifestation of what my brother called "The Creal", that vital metamorphic lava of life as constant creation, we bury our gaze in the poster, the label, the package—like that photo of an anonymous old man Bardo took when he was in London with Ophelia, on the way to Oxford, where her father Peter Lovelace lived.

On the back of the photo, my brother had written:

> *We form ourselves to fit the pattern of the old days, of a time when nothing had yet been discovered on the other side of the limit of reality.*
>
> *We must be ready for another world to emerge, something beyond the daily business agenda. The blank-faced, and the lifeless, shall be buried.*
>
> *Intellect will be considered, sometimes, to collude with what it has denounced, for having sensed such mechanical absurdities, and yet failed to act.*

"Deviaction", for Bardo, was the art of summoning chance. Sort of like this morning, July 27th, 2010: I was wandering in the pine woods that separated the town of Nida from the beach, repeating the word *Life* in my head to keep myself from being contaminated by sadness and discouragement. I picked up a branch with a beak-shaped knot on one end and tossed it into the air without purpose or desire or bitterness. The way you make an offering. The way you let yourself go. I didn't hear the branch hit the ground; it had fallen in such a way as to suspend itself vertically from a thinner branch, dangling a meter above the earth. A knife-thrower couldn't have done it if he tried. It was a small miracle, but it made me feel a flicker of gratitude. I sat down on the forest floor and the images began again, dancing in my head.

It was before dawn on April 21st, 2010, at around two o'clock in the morning. I still hadn't seen the little spirit, when the waiter announced that the Sir Winston was about to close. I offered to spend the night at my brother's place, but he preferred to go home alone, with his mysterious little mobile soul; he was sure, he said, that it was just a hallucination and would be gone in the morning. I insisted on accompanying him out to his Fiat 500, though.

"Are you sure you don't want me to come with you?"

"Don't worry. I'll let you know how things are in the morning."

"Make sure you don't get arrested for corrupting a minor . . ."

When Bardo woke up a few hours later, just after sunrise, he called me first thing to tell me that the child was gone. He seemed torn between relief and disappointment. The little Bernardo apparition had stirred a kind of uneasiness in him, an idea that he might have begun to sell out in the last few years by not devoting himself exclusively enough to the Verb, with the afternoons he spent as an architect. Was he a lost soul, a sham poet? Had he become too subdued since the breakup with Ophelia? Eating breakfast that morning, he wondered if he'd given up on his "childhood dreams" — a term, on second thought, that didn't quite satisfy him. When you're five years old, you don't know enough about the world to want to change it. Or do you?

After breakfast he got dressed and went out, walking the length of the cemetery without the faintest idea that he'd be buried there himself in a few weeks' time. He made his way through the forest to the grazing fields of the stud farm at Jardy, five hundred meters' distance. It was a place that emanated a kind of serenity, maybe because it had been home for centuries to a Benedictine priory. As he often did, Bardo sat down on the white wall of the vast enclosure and watched the horses. As always, he found them soothing—and slightly depressing, with their compulsive grazing. He had sat on this same wall with Ophelia five years ago, he remembered, in March, 2005, shortly before their separation . . .

He gave a start. A little voice had just piped "hello" in his ear. It was the morning of April 21st, 2010, and the spirit-child had reappeared, sitting next to him on the wall and dressed in a translucent T-shirt. With that same insistent gaze as before, that same lilting but determined voice, the boy said:

"You're thinking about her."

After the first, reflexive jolt of fear, my brother found that he was pleased to see the child again. After all, he thought, if he was going mad, this wasn't so bad, as disturbances go. Little Bernardo was a pleasant companion.

Two horses ambled up to the wall of the enclosure. My brother had the impression that they could see the spirit-boy, that they were even drawn to him when he stretched out his hand to pat their noses. Animals seemed very receptive to him.

Bardo summoned up his courage. "Are you my soul?" he asked, again.

"Tell me how you first met."

"Why are you so interested in Ophelia?"

"Is she the woman you've loved most?"

"Yes."

"Well, then."

My brother remembered everything. On the evening they met he had risked his life, dodging speeding traffic in the Place de l'Étoile.

"I wasn't in great shape at the time," he said. "I was pretty depressed. I felt like I didn't have any friends, except for my twin brother. The world seemed more and more like something false, filled with people sleep-walking—I'm sure I was one of them myself. I used to walk up to the Arc de Triomphe every Monday night, trying to find some sense of direction in my future. That little ritual kept me from needing medication or seeing a shrink. The place reinvigorated me, despite how lonely I was—maybe because of its name, which made me think of the triumph of life, rather than war, or Napoleon. The night I met Ophelia it was the very start of spring. A Monday in March."

Bardo paused here, as the horses wandered off in search of fresh tufts of grass. In his surprise at seeing the spirit-boy again, he had forgotten that when he'd awakened the day before, had still been lying in bed, a few moments before the child's first appearance, he had felt vague, blurry. More indistinct than ever. Suddenly, like a promise, or a desire for redemption, the image of a luminous cord had risen up in front of him. He had immediately felt as if he needed to identify himself with this slender line stretching skyward; it was, he thought confusedly, a representation of the best part of himself. The deepest heart of the matter. Just afterward, he had written the lines:

Why do we sing
When everywhere generosity
Lies sleeping?
To stimulate the velocity
Of thread and throne ascending.

And the child had appeared.

"So, what happened?" said the boy.

Bardo jumped down from the wall and began to walk again, followed by little Bernardo, who took his hand. My brother picked up his story again, looking straight ahead.

"I'd just arrived at the foot of the narrow spiral staircase that goes up to the roof of the Arc de Triomphe. I know I was feeling very serious and staring off into the distance, but I guess from the outside there was nothing very remarkable about me. At almost the exact same moment, on the other side of Paris, a tall, half-English girl with hennaed hair was walking between the tombs in Père-Lachaise Cemetery with a bouquet of red-and-white-striped roses—Brocéliande roses—in her hand."

The spirit-child listened. They plunged into the woods, taking a path that curved in an arc behind the cemetery.

After that, my brother resigned himself to the odd little presence. Bernardo still refused to say where had come from. Sometimes he disappeared for days, showing up again whenever Bardo thought about Ophelia. But on May 7th, 2010, the spirit-boy did more than just listen. He made a suggestion.

"What if you went to Hamburg, to see her again?"

8

By chance

Nothing ever starts at a single given point in a biography, but since there has to be a point A in Bardo and Ophelia's story, let's say it's A for the Arc de Triomphe. On that March evening in 2004, my brother, with his downcast air and distant gaze, had just reached the top of the metal stairs that spiralled up to the monument's roof. From that starry promontory, you can contemplate all four cardinal points of the cityscape around you, and search the skies for the North Star.

That panoramic view, the certainty that he wouldn't bump into anyone he knew on the platform, the triumphal air of the place—the vitalist ritual of the ascendance, maybe—none of it fully explained why Bardo was compelled to go there every Monday night: there was also his hope of conquering the vertigo from which he suffered, through repeated exposure to the possibility of jumping.

Part of him was attracted by the void. Seduced, even, by the idea of a suicide that would consist of yielding to the siren force of gravity. Visitors to the top of the Arc are protected from the fifty meters that separate them from *terra firma* by nothing more than a row of vertical bars over which an agile and determined body could climb in a matter of seconds.

On that night, Bardo approached the guardrail with a step he would have liked to be just a bit firmer. His eyes were drawn irresistibly to the street below, where the cars were the size of his hand. He was troubled by the possibility of jumping, as easy as it would be irreversible. The same is true of so much in our lives. Destruction and failure always seem to be within arm's reach, while to stay in a state of exaltation and wonderment, much less to reach the sacred point of no relapse, is difficult beyond expression.

His gaze picked out the pyramid of the Louvre in the distance and then glided back up the Champs-Élysées, from the place de la Concorde to the foot of the Arc. He breathed deeply from his diaphragm, to dispel the panic. If someone had told him he was suicidal, he would have denied it—but sometimes, back then, even when doing something as simple as looking around him or smoking a cigarette, he was seized by a feeling of terror mingled with an irrational tinge of guilt. By the sense that, everywhere, a tragedy of cosmic proportions was playing out. Or he would abruptly realize that he had real admiration for almost nothing anymore; that everything was slowly flattening out like a Cartesian plane.

From his perch atop the Arc he looked down again at the ground, full of pedestrians who suddenly seemed so vulnerable. He felt as if he were shrinking, becoming extremely tiny himself. Could his impulse to jump stem from the need to adjust his aspirations, to make them more modest? Should he maybe lower his standards, his ambitions, and *come back to earth*?

Be more *realistic*? Betray his ideals? When we were younger, my brother and I had played a game in which we told each other the more-or-less imaginary life stories of some of history's greatest adventures. My master was the navigator Magellan. Bardo's was Shakespeare.

I remember that, a few days before he met Ophelia, Bardo had been entranced by a new biography of *Hamlet*'s author which he'd found on display in a bookstore. It was a massive tome of more than six hundred pages, but the narrator had been too exhaustive, attempting so painstakingly to dissect every single (wildly divergent) theory about the Shakespearean myth that any semblance of the living man was drowned in a sea of detail. Yet, there were a few passages in the book that retained their fascination. One of them addressed a rumor that there was an original version of *Romeo and Juliet* that had been judged heretical and censored by the Elizabethan church, particularly because it included a troubling secret. The legend claimed that three or four lines spoken by Friar Laurence had been deleted, lines that spoke of looking another person in the eyes for eight hundred and eighty-eight breaths.

That was all the biography had said on the subject, but in 2004 this had been enough to plunge my brother into a state of depression. No woman had ever said "I love you" to him while looking deep into his eyes. In fact, he had decided somewhat exaggeratedly, we seemed to be living in a time when women never said "I love you" anymore.

Bardo stared downwards. His vision blurred. He felt his body shrivelling, and a faint groan of pain rose in his chest, accompanied by an intense feeling of fragility. It was like a sense of injustice that seemed to want to push him out of society altogether; if he wanted to keep his dignity, a voice whispered, he should withdraw from it entirely—eliminate himself completely—just to go one better than this world, with its incessant suggestions that he wasn't suited for it. Tears prickled in his eyes. His fingers gripped the metal bar. *Arc de Triomphe*, he thought, grimacing.

He turned, and watched the couples blissfully taking photos. No doubt they would use the images to comfort themselves, to remind themselves that they weren't ghosts, without realizing that they were contributing to their own evaporation by taking part in such clichés. It was the last way of feeling *present*: looking at the world from the perspective of photography—that is, of nostalgia.

His intimacy with the void now disrupted, my brother decided to descend. In a few moments he was walking along the path that circles the Arc.

Then he saw her.

She had just come up the avenue de Wagram on a big black bicycle and was negotiating the intersection, her face slightly pink with the effort. Her fiery hair kept whipping across her eyes. Pedaling with her back held very straight, she came within a few meters of Bardo. She was glorious, like a manifestation of the sunset.

Their eyes met briefly. He was so deeply moved that he felt thankfulness. She was already receding into the distance. After an instant's hesitation, he went after her, heedless of the cars, the blaring horns and squealing brakes. He was a joyous madman, crossing the most dangerous square in the city at a run. Catching up to her, he turned and, swaggeringly, jogged backward alongside her.

"Hello!" he called.

"Good evening." Her response was cool.

"Where are you going?" persisted Bardo, between breaths.

"Nowhere."

"Where have you come from?"

"Père-Lachaise Cemetery."

"Why?"

"My twin sister is there. Or rather, not there."

My brother slowed down and switched directions, going forward again. A driver honked his horn. She stood up on the pedals of her bicycle, as if preparing to ride away from my brother. He had just enough time to gather his wits and call:

"Give me a first name!"

She slowed down, seemed to hesitate for an instant. Then:

"I'm named after the girl who killed herself in *Hamlet*. What about you?"

"I . . ."

Ophelia, who had stopped pedaling, stared at Bardo. His eyes were filled with tears. She smiled.

"You can tell me next time."

She disappeared into the night. A few days later they met again, by chance.

9

I'm dangerous

Over the last three months I've often looked at the Khnopff mask on the front of Bardo's postcard, as if the winged face were my twin's. There is something both encouraging and lonely in its eyes. My relationship with Bardo was so rich that neither of us had very many friends. I work from home as a translator, which means I don't have colleagues, either. My first venture out into Parisian society after Bardo's death wasn't until June 2nd, 2010.

After having dinner with my parents for the last time before their return to Portugal, a call from an acquaintance convinced me to go to a literary awards ceremony, where I could at least pretend to think about something else. It was at the Brasserie Vaudeville, and I recognized a few vaguely erudite gray-hairs I'd worked for in the past. Publishing is no nastier an industry than any other; some of its members are spiteful snobs or spineless cowards who sit in paper houses throwing sugar water as if it were fire, but that's true everywhere. There are also those who have stayed strong in their quest to help poetry and thought take flight and soar above a sea of simple mimicry.

I was standing alone in the center of the brasserie. I started to feel ill, as if I were drowning in the hub-bub of voices. Waiters were passing platters of sushi. I felt an urge to retch at the indifference and ugliness of a place where Bardo could never again burst smiling through the doors. The whole world was nothing more than a cardboard diorama. I prepared to flee.

Suddenly, a nearby woman lost her balance and stepped on my foot. It was Annabelle, whom I hadn't spoken to since that evening on the terrace of the Café des Philosophes. I stared at her. "Thanks," I managed to croak.

"Sorry! I bet you think I did it on purpose. Hey, you've got tears in your eyes. Did I hurt you?"

"No. It isn't that."

"What is it, then?"

"I'm allergic to sushi."

I was struck by her gaze, which seemed more lively than it had last time. Behind her rather cool appearance she exuded a character that surprised me, that I thought might soothe me. I could have taken her in my arms and wept. But because I stayed silent, she said something about needing to "get back to her friend." Another woman walking out of my life before she'd even come in.

I left without saying goodbye to anyone. A little over half an hour later I reached the front garden of the studio in Ville d'Avray. It was completely dark. I looked up at the sky, dotted with infinitesimal white pinpricks. Not a gleam of hope. I knew I'd wake up again the next day with the same block of sadness lodged in my chest, the same feeling—maybe more intense than ever—that I'd never experience pure joy. Can you come to terms with being only half alive?

Now, a month and a half later, in the isolation of this Lithuanian near-island, the block of sadness is still there, though its edges have been softened a bit by the calm of my surroundings. And the same thought keeps rising again and again to the surface of my mind, despite all my efforts to keep it submerged: what if the football fan at the Sternschanze metro station wasn't what he seemed? What if the 'accident' was really deliberate—even premeditated—murder?

My brother never mentioned anyone to me who might have hated him that much. Tomorrow I'll call the Hamburg police again, even though I'm starting to think they're never going to find the person responsible. And that I might never find Ophelia.

In the depths of her eyes, when she first came into Bardo's life, there were—if one of my brother's poems is to be believed—"mountains of fire that rumbled beneath the feet of the soldiers of an invisible army." Her moods were often unpredictable, because she couldn't help aspiring to an existence in which every moment would be exhilarating and surprising, and would prove to her that fate was finally smiling down on her. A way of running away, maybe.

When she met my brother, Paris was new territory for her. A place of exile. And, she hoped, one that might save her from the compulsion that had already caused her so much self-loathing: she had an uncontrollable need to lie.

Bardo only figured out gradually, and at his own expense, that half of what Ophelia said to him was either distorted or completely made up. If he'd known it earlier he might never have fallen in love with her, but it wasn't until after their time in Portugal that he realized just how deep her tendency to mix falsehood with reality actually ran. And by then, he was so deeply in love with her that he could only feel compassion for her; it was clear to him that this falseness wasn't deliberate, that it was almost a kind of psychosis, a chronic behaviour that didn't reflect the truth of Ophelia's soul. She didn't lie because she was bored, or because she was playing games, or had an overactive imagination, or was malicious. No, when she lied it was probably because she was rebelling against a violent past she never talked about. I'm convinced that Bardo loved Ophelia because she gave him the opportunity to fight for love, to make it triumph over dishonesty. Did he win the fight before he died? If his last postcard could be believed, maybe he did.

I'm also fighting a battle against anger. As long as Bardo was alive, I could hang on. Our union made this world acceptable, sometimes even entertaining. Am I going to turn into a lone wolf? I've run out of tears. And when I don't write I feel empty, hollowed out. This story is what's keeping me tethered to life.

And I'm not trying to go at my story full-force, either, the way an experienced storyteller would. You have to know how to wander.

Because the end just might be my undoing.

This morning, I see that Ophelia has replied to my text. Cryptically. *Better not to follow me. I'm dangerous.*

10

Atop the silent dunes

Here on the Courland Isthmus on July 27th, 2010, just before midnight, bathed in the light of the moon and the stars, I think back again to the incident with the branch that stayed suspended in the air, like a totem. I come back to the present alone, on the high dune of Parnidis, which they sometimes call the Lithuanian Sahara even though it represents only the tiniest portion of a desert.

My feet savour the softness of the night-dampened sand. Up here the scents of pine trees and the sea mingle in the air; the strong line of the horizon is barely visible. The wind is cool rather than cold. I sit down on this natural promontory, and for the first time since my brother's death I feel free of hate, almost serene.

Behind me, a hundred meters downhill, people are sleeping in the wooden houses that border the lagoon. The isthmus is only just over a kilometer wide at this point. I look straight ahead, just making out the treetops in the darkness. I think about the fact that a fairly short distance from here, just an hour away by car, is the city of Kaliningrad, the former Königsberg, birthplace of Kant, where he wrote in 1788: "Two things fill my mind with ever new and increasing admiration and awe, the oftener and more steadily I reflect on them: the starry heavens above me and the moral law within me."

My breathing slows.

And Bardo appears to me.

He is like a giant filling the valley before me, the image of a Bardo formed of sparkling nocturnal light. He seems to smile, as he says:

"I didn't die in vain."

Tears fill my eyes; I can't formulate either an answer or a question. He continues, cheerfully:

"Be joyful. Be proud."

"Why? Were you murdered?"

"Yes. But I also sought out this death. I was already looking for it, in a confused sort of way, when I went to test my vertigo on the top of the Arc de Triomphe. And now I know why."

"*Why?*"

"So that I could announce a birth."

I don't speak. My brain is shooting out panic signals. Have I gone so crazy with grief over time that I've reached the point of hallucinating? Bardo interrupts my ratiocinations.

"You have to forget the vagaries of our life stories."

"What are you *talking* about? *Who killed you?*"

"Thousands of humans start to go through metamorphosis, but the pull of banality is too strong. Sometimes the child doesn't survive the birth process—again. The risk of failure, the convenience of habit, the comfort of being stuck in the mud . . . all of them favour the dreamless sleep."

"I have so many questions. Ophelia . . ."

"I'm leaving you to find Ophelia, and to love her instead of hating her. And our son Bernardo, who is no ghost—you have to protect him."

"Your son? Tell me who killed you!"

Bardo's image began to fade away.

"Don't leave me!"

"I'm not leaving you. I'm right behind you, every-where you go."

And the gleaming form melted back into the stars, leaving me stunned and alone atop the silent dunes.

11

With Bardo's son

In Paris, fortunately, no one knew her. Because she'd always seemed older than she actually was, she had been lucky in her exile; barely a week after her arrival in January 2004, two months before she met Bardo, she'd landed a job teaching conversational English at a private school for high school students with academic problems (rather than financial ones) on the west side, a few minutes by bicycle from the Arc de Triomphe. Shortly thereafter, thanks to a letter from the school's director, she'd managed to rent a small flat nearby on the rue Bois-le-Vent without parental permission. Her father didn't even know she was hiding in France.

At least, that's what she'd thought at the time.

The apartment was no more than twenty square meters in size, but she felt safer there than she had ever done before. She hoped, at the time, to find happiness through a chance encounter, to find truth in a feeling more intense than the everyday ones—but these desires were brief and her freedom, she feared, was conditional. It wasn't that unusual, she told herself, trying to boost her own spirits, to have your life cut off at twenty. Her father had let her go without too much protest, maybe because she'd seemed so determined to break her silence. The Oxford professor couldn't allow a scandal that might harm his reputation.

It was fear that had kept her from fleeing for so long; fear and the habit of submission, and guilt, and maybe even, she told herself, the masochistic pleasure of self-flagellation. But above all, it had been the desire to protect her brother William. At twelve years old, and afflicted with severe mental retardation, he was even more vulnerable than she to the tyrannical figure of a father who treated him as a half-wit and a slave. She hated herself sometimes for leaving him. He'd cried on her shoulder a lot.

Bardo didn't find out about any of this until months after they met, when they visited Peter Lovelace at the end of September, 2004. And even then, Ophelia lied so much that when she spoke in veiled terms about incest he consoled her, but not without suspicion. Later, when she revealed that her mother had committed suicide because she could no longer stand watching her husband abuse their daughter, Bardo, shocked, wondered if this wasn't yet another distortion of reality. Ophelia was like a hunted soul, forever creating decoys.

In that Parisian late winter of 2004, during Ophelia's darker moments, the future seemed to her like creeping brown mold invading an old wall and rotting the wallpaper. A more creative view might have seen those spots as a sign, a dancing silhouette that heralded a new world behind the ruins. Hadn't she been able to hold on to that attitude? No, she told herself. Ophelia was sick of the future. Her efforts to control the train of time always failed; in fact, they led all too often to a derailment. But, if my brother were to be believed, deep in her eyes there was still "a mysterious reflection of the rain and the earth."

On some days, her confidence came back in bursts of tenderness for little things: a student's smile, the memory of the funny faces her brother used to pull, riding her bicycle along the banks of the Seine. She could veer from despondency to euphoria in a matter of seconds, but most of the time she simply struggled along, tangled in the spider webs that concealed her inner monsters. It was a fragile balance, nearly an impossible one.

People she met often detected in her eyes the smolder of those who have seen too much. Some were repelled by it, while others were drawn to her intensity as if hypnotized—and those people she tended, despite herself, to shred between her teeth, to tear to pieces so that she would not begin to love them. The ones you loved died, or betrayed you.

After school, in the evenings, she often went to visit the grave of her mother, Lucie, a French woman who, thirty years earlier, had had the misfortune to study for a PhD on Shakespeare at Oxford and to fall in love with her supervisor, a stern and elegant man who could talk well about interesting things. He was among the world's foremost experts on the author of *Hamlet*. Lucie's final wish, at least, had been respected by Peter Lovelace; she had asked to be buried in the family vault in Paris.

Ophelia's strongest memory of her mother was of the summer preceding her death, when the family had taken a holiday in Lithuania, on the Courland Isthmus. They had rented a wooden cottage in Nida, and for a brief moment everything had seemed all right. Peter had appeared determined to act only as a father; William acted almost like all the other boys, and Lucie was radiant. Hell had stayed behind in England. But it had still been there, waiting, when they got back.

A few days after the beautiful happenstance at the Arc de Triomphe, Bardo was on the metro, reading the beginning of Act III of *Hamlet*, when he heard a voice say, in an English accent:

"So you do know my name."

Absorbed in his reading, he hadn't noticed her approach. She sat down next to him, her shoulder touching his. He looked at her face, close-up this time, and was rewarded with a smile that already seemed knowing, somehow. She stood up. The train slowed to a stop, while Bardo's heart beat faster. He felt a rush of blood warming his shoulders and torso. She smiled at him again, more sombrely this time.

"Shakespeare is my real father."

"Ophelia, wait! Come and have a coffee with me."

"I'm English. I'd rather have tea. What's your name?"

"Bardo."

"Are you following me, Bardo? You should be running away."

"Why? This is the second time we've met by chance. Don't you believe in dest—"

She pressed a finger to my brother's lips. "Shhh. I believe in inevitability. Do you know the song? *Je suis malade, complètement malade . . .*"

The sliding doors of the train car separated them. She melted into the crowd thronging the République metro station, escaping again like a flying fish. The expression on Bardo's face was more suggestive of "damn carp!" than *carpe diem*, but he gathered himself enough to get off the train at the next station and double back, only to spend a few minutes loitering in the place de la République with his volume of *Hamlet* as a consolation prize . . .

Six years have passed since then. It's dawn on the thirty-first of July, 2010, and I'm still in Nida. I called Inspector Kreiss yesterday. They still haven't identified the Fulham fan.

I'm sure they'll never find him.

It's seven o'clock. I'm sitting at the foot of a pine tree. You can hear the sea.

I'm rereading a letter from my twin, dated October 10th, 2005, four months after the breakup:

> *In the depths of your eyes, Ophelia, dust formed whirlpools of expectation. Horns sounded a fox-hunt of timeouts.*
>
> *You painted trompe-l'oeils everywhere and I watched you do it, half taken in, always wondering what miracle had brought you here, right here, instead of only in my head.*
>
> *You looked like a little girl sometimes. I'd never loved like that, with so much compassion and polychromy, such fond blindness, and even avidity.*
>
> *I used to say before I met you that I was evolving in a purgatory of rough drafts. There are times in life when everything is plunged into resistance, the dam of what should have been able to flow freely.*

We've turned into that red interlacing around the white circle that you painted a few weeks after we met at Lea-Maria Spielswehk's studio; a little polyurethane, some oil, an old newspaper, a bit of charcoal and lacquer, a scrap of linen, and the stem of a Brocéliande rose. I've learned to look at you.

You were light in the shadowy places.

Could we have avoided this day, when we walk in the Parc de Saint-Cloud, separated and nearly dead?

The curtain has fallen on the four poles, madder, the crossroads of the Étoile, the sound of your voice to the east, the perfume of your paint-stained fingers to the south, the honey of your skin to the north, the color of your tears to the west. Our gazes in the center. But not enough time for eight hundred and eighty-eight breaths.

I thought our passion would go further.
That it would give birth to a world.
Was I wrong?

It's eight o'clock in the morning. I'm walking on a nearly-deserted beach on the western side of the isthmus. The sea is swirling around my bare feet. I spread my arms, ready to give myself up, to unburden myself of the litanies rotting my brain. In my pocket, my telephone vibrates.

It's a message from Ophelia. "My father might have guessed I was in Nida. I'm headed north, towards Tallinn, with Bardo's son."

12

From the past into the future

Bardo read *Hamlet* in English soon after meeting Ophelia for the first time. The book seemed to him like a musical bridge to a mysterious and unique world. These were fleshly sentences molded out of the clay of desire, to be listened to even before they could be understood. They took life deep in his gut, intoxicating. Disturbing.

One March evening in 2004, just before sunset, he had gone to sit in the grass on the edge of the stud-farm pastures in Jardy, alone except for the horses snorting softly in the distance. Seated near an oak tree, he had watched the sunlight slide across its leaves. Playfully repeating the phrase "To be, or not to be?" in his mind, he gradually became aware of a sensation of warmth high in his solar plexus. *To be!* It was a feeling of gratitude, almost of freedom.

That was how Bardo lived. The singing of birds perched in the pine trees in his garden usually woke him before eight o'clock. Sometimes one of them emitted a screech that sounded just like an old typewriter. A green woodpecker? My brother would leap out of bed and throw open the shutters, taking a deep breath of chlorophyll and mist. Dazzled by the early morning light, he would inhale the atmosphere that never failed to move and surprise him with its sharp green notes. A few days earlier, in the forest, he had stumbled upon a deer that had looked straight into his eyes for a moment before bounding away. To what extent, he wondered, is the world as we perceive it just a reflection of our own inner landscape? Would a wounded deer become a stag, or continue to leap into death?

A life without natural spaces, lacking the lifeblood of the earth, he thought, couldn't possibly be felt as intensely as one that did—unless it was enhanced by artifice and tics like the forgetting of self, the inconstancy to be found in cigarettes and alcohol and drownings in glasses of water. The previous evening he had seen a young woman sitting on one of the terraces that lined the main boulevards, sucking on a tube of pink lipstick with an air of both pleasure and guilt. This was her little mechanical drug, used the way other people touch the blank screens of their telephones every five minutes. Bardo always said that in the cities we were just like rats, scurrying and biting in our tiny holes. Or sailors passing through the fog just alongside an idyllic island, haunted by the possibility of the shipwreck that could save them. Acting carefree to hide the heaviness of our thoughts. Using smiles as excuses, counting friendships, each of us hoping to find—and hold on to—that person who will say to us: *Call me but love, and I'll be new baptized.*

The vast garden overlooked by the window of the studio in Ville-d'Avray; the thin, determined song of the birds; the ashy scent of the pines; the nocturnal fights of feral cats; the slightly stupid indolence of the horses—this world seemed to him like a dyke, holding back the asphalt and keeping mineral technology away. This semi-rurality gave the misleading impression of solitude while reinforcing his tendency to isolate himself. Sometimes he found himself embracing the tree trunks in the forest.

Once a week, usually on the weekend, I went to see him in his retreat. In the depths of Bardo's eyes there was a man wandering in the desert. Was he going anywhere? In one of the poems he wrote during that time, to which he glued a photo of a blank billboard, he wrote:

> *Does the marching man know where*
>   *he is going?*
> *Or is he a fool asking for the impossible —*
>   *for the desert to bear fruit?*
> *Hordes wither away. Words waver. Phenomena*
>   *are dashed against shopfront windows.*
> *The obsolete crowd will be absent from its*
>   *own burial, dancing in the cemetery of*
>   *spirits, atonic, aphonic, crying out.*
> *To the doubtful, we must say:*
> *Drink your blood—your thirst will pass!*

I've read that last line a hundred times since Bardo died.

It gives me courage.

I'm hoping to meet up with Ophelia in Tallinn soon, if she doesn't change her mind. And Bernardo, who can speak with his father remotely, in the form of a spirit-child. When did my brother realize that he had a son? It can only have been a few hours before his death.

Before leaving Nida, I look out over the valley from the top of Parnidis Dune—hoping, maybe, to hear Bardo's voice again. Later, lower, I end up in front of the stick balanced on its branch, and dream of my spirit being able to scatter like my twin's, and dissolve amid the riot of leaves. To become the forest. But for now, my fate is to leave Lithuania for Estonia . . . the country of astonishment?

I'm sure Bardo was astonished, six years earlier, on that early April day in 2004 when he had his third chance encounter with Ophelia, this time on the Pont-Neuf.

She had just come from the Pont des Arts, watching the pedestrians pass at varying speeds, attracted by this minimalist wood-and-metal footbridge where adolescents gathered to loiter by the dozen. A few minutes earlier she had paused in front of the window of an art gallery on the rue de Seine, glimpsing the reflection of her own silhouette between the paintings. The image reminded her a bit of the little girl she remembered having been once. Shadows drifted across the brilliance of the face. She would have loved for everything to burst back into color, like in the painting in the window that was superimposed over her own face, a kaleidoscope of vivid tones. A small card at the bottom of the painting gave its title and the artist's name: *Mirabilia*, by Lea-Maria Spielswehk.

Ophelia drew closer to the Pont-Neuf, turning her face up to the sun for a moment, closing her eyes and basking in its warmth, caught between an undefinable sense of hope and the desire to abandon her escape and go back to England. To protect William. But too many horrible images lingered in her head, tearing at her. She didn't have enough control over her own mind yet. She went to stand at the guardrail, gazing out at the Seine.

The water flowed with the same intensity on both sides, she noted, with only the tiniest of variations here and there, but to the west of the bridge, in the distance, was the ocean, where all was lost—while somewhere to the east was the source, where everything still seemed possible. Should she swim against the current, or let herself be carried by it? Go back to the source, to the time before death. Move in reverse, flow along, or stay in equilibrium, there on the bridge? Sometimes she felt as if she couldn't bear her own body any more, that battered flesh, victimized for too long. She lifted her head and looked toward the Louvre museum. Felt that there was no choice but to go north.

Behind her, she heard Bardo's voice. She turned, saw the shock in his eyes. She cried out:

"Are you following me?"

"How could I be?" protested my brother.

How could she believe that chance had brought them together for the third time? She seemed furious, and started to walk away. He wasn't sure whether to follow her. But he felt that there wouldn't be a fourth encounter unless he seized this chance. There was a sudden burst of nasal, bombastic sound; a brass band had begun crossing the bridge in the opposite direction. The world seemed made of nothing but stimuli. Ophelia felt an urge to smile, and was annoyed with herself for having been unfriendly.

The brass band—it was made up of students—came closer, clanging. My brother explained loudly that he almost never took this bridge. He had just come from L'Ecume des Pages, a bookstore in the Saint-Germain quarter, and was just wandering aimlessly. He had seen Ophelia from the back first, but hadn't believed it could be her.

"Do you often follow girls in the street?"

"Occasionally, why not."

"Well, that's an honest answer, at least."

"Weren't you following me the other day, on the metro?"

"I'm not that desperate."

"I would never follow anyone out of desperation, just admiration." He gestured at the quay, on the Louvre side. "We could go down and walk on the embankment. It's quieter."

Their hands brushed. She had stopped listening. She looked around, fighting a renewed wave of panic. Her breathing had turned harsh. She went down with him to the paved embankment, caught in the grip of confused emotion.

He spoke. The city took on color again, the gray of the facades vanishing like dead skin. From closer up, the river looked different as well. It seemed less controlled and less threatening, all at the same time. Crystalline sparks glinted here and there on the surface of the water. Ophelia allowed herself to be mesmerized by them. It was as if these glitters were disregarding the unilateral flow of the river, sparkling in all directions, carving out a thin layer of desire just above the unfathomable. She kept her eyes open until dazzled tears turned the river into a kind of starry beehive. Tears of joy, tears that drained her spirit of its unremitting grief. Bardo sat beside her, silent.

Stay here, she whispered to herself, feeling a sense of calm come over her. *Stay here where you feel the freedom to dance with the water, where you can forget that destiny doesn't always compensate people for their losses. Don't think about the sea, where everything fades away. Stop seeing the source anywhere but right here, right now. Bury yourself in the moment, to fight the Enemy.* The swirling of the Seine intensified. A wave dashed against the quay. Bardo had drawn closer to her. Too close.

She remembered, suddenly, that she had a body that attracted idiots. With an abrupt movement, she jerked to her feet, tossing a "Goodbye" over her shoulder, her voice almost a scream.

"What are you afraid of?" Bardo was yelling too.

"You," she answered, with a snatch of sardonic laughter.

But her steps had already slowed down.

"You," he echoed her.

He had caught up with her. "You sparkle like this river," he said, gently.

She heard herself laugh. She looked at Bardo's face; it was clear-eyed, innocent. He held her gaze. "You seem a bit . . . lost. Does it have anything to do with your twin sister in Père-Lachaise?"

She smiled bitterly. "You ask too many questions."

"Why did you say, on the metro, that you were sick?"

"Because it's true."

"Is it psychological?"

She made a childlike movement with her head, something between *yes* and *no*, which he would see often in the months to come.

"Don't push me. You'll regret it. Go back up on the bridge and forget me."

"I'm not scared."

She looked at him, suddenly very serious. Her eyes were wet, her voice steely. "You should be afraid."

"Why?"

"Your questions are really starting to bug me. I have leukaemia, okay?"

Bardo's face was stunned. "Leukaemia? Cancer?"

"Chronic myeloid leukaemia. It's a cancer of the blood. I found out a month ago. I've got six months to live, at most. See? We're deep into pathos, here. Now leave me alone."

"But . . ."

"Please."

"All right—but at least take my number." She took the large card Bardo held out; it was a postcard showing the Arc de Triomphe. He had written his phone number on the back. She climbed the stairs toward the Louvre without looking back, her heart thumping.

The further she got away from my brother, the more she imagined what it would have been like if she'd just talked to him more nicely, more directly. There was nothing rational about her compulsion to run from him; there had been nothing in his smile, or the tone of his voice, or his eyes. Why did she feel as if she'd been cut in half, separated from herself? In her imagination, she confided to him that she was more than a little bit lost. That she wasn't afraid of herself, so much as of her father. That she didn't really know how she felt about anything anymore, and that her coolness was a way of pretending to be coherent. She felt, at twenty years old, like a broken machine, a scattered kaleidoscope, a character on a quest for some lofty ideal. She was only herself when she wasn't thinking about the past, and those times had become very rare.

She was just wandering Paris aimlessly, at a time when other girls were starting to get their bearings, when some of them were even already establishing their own happy little kingdoms, surrounded by friendship and laughter and acceptable love.

She turned around. Bardo was gone.

Without warning, the face of a young man appeared in her imagination with the beauty of a revelation. Could he have touched something vital in her, with so few words, in so short a time?

Suddenly unsteady on her feet, she sat down on a bench and cried.

And then she remembered the postcard in her pocket, that might be—could be—a doorway for her, from the past into the future.

13

She agreed to see me

At first, hardly anyone paid attention to the red-headed young woman sitting on the ground near the Louvre pyramid on that spring day in 2004.

A few kids pointed at her, asking their fathers why she was crying. Ophelia stayed there for hours, unmoving, giving way here and there to fresh bursts of tears. Awful memories assaulted her until she was teetering on the edge of panic—but she fought with everything she had to keep herself from interpreting them, looking from time to time at Bardo's postcard with its photo of the Arc de Triomphe, trying to remind herself that reality was not unalterable, that she was more than just the product of her past. What made her the saddest now weren't the nightmares inherited from her father, but the absurdity of her days, the solitude, the compulsion to lie to everyone. Why had she told Bardo she had leukaemia?

After two hours she managed to let go enough to abandon herself to the moment, to observing the more or less animated forms that surrounded her, and she started to feel the beginnings of calmness. She felt as if cracks were beginning to appear in the glass bubble encasing her mind—that maybe she *could* discover the world, project her feelings onto it, read signs in it. She saw, now, that all these murmurings of existence around her were tracing lines that intersected, diverged, drew closer together, with various degrees of consciousness. *We are pierced through,* she thought. *I can say: I'm sad, I'm happy, I'm angry, I think this or that—but maybe all these thoughts and feelings are barely traveling through our bodies.*

She had the feeling that her entire life had been leading to that spot in front of the Louvre, as if the universe had been reeling her in. She felt drunk; she had been sitting on the ground without moving for hours. That wasn't like her. It was out of character, unusual. Maybe soon some powerful force would transport her somewhere else, but for now it felt like nowhere else existed anymore. Finally she smiled, thinking: *I'm here. Everything is right here.*

The tears gave way to an expression that spoke of both serenity and defiance. Occasionally a passer-by spoke to her, asked if she was all right. She didn't answer; only smiled. She watched, with a kind of gratitude, the last reflections of the setting sun on the glass of the pyramid.

Shortly thereafter, a middle-aged woman, a natural redhead, sat down next to Ophelia without speaking. She had a small tattoo—a word—on her forehead, in the third-eye spot.

"I like to come and sit here too," she said eventually. "On the axis between the obelisk in the Place de la Concorde and the Arc de Triomphe. It's a sort of fertility rite."

There was something gentle, maternal, in the face and voice of this stranger. "I'm called Lea-Maria Spielswehk," she said. "It's a pseudonym."

Sometimes, when you look at a mirror from a certain angle, it's like there is water on the other side, and you could dive into it. This was the effect the spirit-boy had on my brother, when the latter talked about Ophelia's past. Little Bernardo listened gravely, and occasionally asked a question.

"Who is she, this Spitzweck?"

"Spielswehk. She's quite a well-known artist; her work is shown in a lot of places. Her pseudonym is an anagram of William Shakespeare."

"Did she really have a tattoo on her forehead?"

"Yes. The word *fire*, in English."

The child made a face somewhere between disgust and astonishment.

Léopoldine Spiel, alias Lea-Maria Spielswehk, was a conceptual artist originally from Switzerland. Her first successes had come in the early nineties, especially the time she painted an Alfa Romeo pink and renamed it Juliet. Or when, during the night of 14 July 1993, without authorization, she planted pigs' heads on pikes in the center of the Place de la Bastille, under a banner which read *A Midsummer Night's Dream*. More recently, on February 29th, 2003, then aged forty-six and well enough known on the international art scene that she didn't (in theory) have to seek out attention anymore, Spielswehk had had the word *fire* tattooed in purple ink on her forehead. The operation had taken several hours, as the skin of the forehead is very delicate and extreme caution had been necessary. The result was exact, and oddly elegant.

"I wouldn't want that," said the spirit-child.

My brother smiled. "Forehead tattoos are nothing new in human history, you know. Polynesian warriors did it for centuries. They declared their relationships to one another by marking their foreheads."

In an April 2003 interview with *Le Temps*, Spielswehk justified her action in a somewhat strange way: "We have become slaves to our own heads, our own brains, to a reductionist way of thinking. They've taken over passion and spirit, sense and signs. How does a brain think? It functions according to a very simple value system: everything that is lower than it in the body is inferior. The feet are at the bottom of the scale. Our feet often hurt, they're often ugly; especially the feet of other people. All they can do is walk the straight and narrow—because of that, they're useful. Higher up, and a little better than the feet because they bring pleasure, are the sexual organs. But they're inferior too, because they're obsessional. They keep the brain from thinking up its power strategies, and they're a source of frustration and misunderstanding. The hands are the head's best accomplices, as we all know, but they are servile and impatient. And further up still there is the mouth, which allows us to speak. But the mouth itself, which so often speaks in order to say nothing, or to say things we regret later, is inferior to the eyes, which know how to look in silence, and to the ears, which can be spies.

"Today, thanks to neuroscience, we are witnessing the final attack of the brain on the rest of the body and, even worse, on the mind, which was thought to animate the body up 'til now. The thinking brain is being pulled further and further apart from the raving, disorganized spirit.

"But brains without spirit have no heart. They don't believe in the vital fire of life. They do nothing but manage the everyday. Which doesn't mean that we should be simplistic, and write off the brain altogether. Hearts without brains sometimes lack common sense. The main thing is: not to make ourselves complicit in the victory of our brains over our spiritual flesh—that would be vengeance, not victory. That's what my tattoo means: "Free yourself from brain-slavery!""

My brother walked with Bernardo through the forest. The child asked:

"So Ophelia called you after the third time you met?"

"Yes. But not until about three weeks later. She was just about to leave her studio and move into Spielswehk's. She'd become her assistant. It was there, on April 20th, 2004, finally, that she agreed to see me."

14

The horizon was suddenly aflame

Bus by bus, I came back north through the misty Lithuanian countryside. Urbanization hasn't yet done its dirty work there in those rugged plains. Wooden houses; old bicycles with fierce-faced riders; interminable, vaguely-cultivated fields; and ruined villages: violence, and gentleness. It's when you're abroad that you really understand the deafness of the world, like a rumbling threat.

It's now Sunday morning, August 1st, 2010. I'm in a cheap hotel in Riga (I'm going to have to watch my spending if I want to keep travelling). I'm writing this on the balcony of a tiny room that gives out onto a tiled roof. There's always a church dome on the horizon. Tomorrow I'm catching a bus to Tallinn. In less than five hours I'll be with Ophelia—if she's really waiting for me there.

How long will it take her to work up the courage to see me? Does the little boy know his father is dead? He has to, surely. Maybe he and Bardo are still having their talks, out there somewhere . . . perhaps on some starry promontory? I take the wooden kaleidoscope out of my bag, and my eyes fill with tears. It must have been a last-minute present for little Bernardo.

After flipping through the pages of a brochure on the area around Riga, I leave the museum-filled streets of the old city, take the Soviet-era tram number 11, and get off a few kilometers away on the shores of Lake Kisezers. Kids are swimming in the green water. I pass more than one pretty girl, but I don't have it in me to flirt with them. I would have liked to play around, to explore a little, but my mind keeps flip-flopping between confusion and preoccupation, slashed through with the anguished desire to understand how, in just a few months, I've managed to end up alone in the middle of this bizarre tragedy. It's like a clouding of the will, a withering of airiness, an ordeal that seems insurmountable, and nothing makes any sense at all to me except the nearness, finally, of the woman my brother loved, and the responsibility of knowing that he has a son. Is it sensible to meet up with Ophelia? And what if she really is dangerous—so dangerous that everyone who gets close to her ends up in a coffin?

Lea-Maria Spielswehk died on May 6th, 2006, of a brain tumor—at least, that was the official story. She had, it seems, fallen in love with Ophelia. Shortly after they met, the artist abandoned installations and started painting in oils again, creating multiple imaginary neo-Symbolist portraits of Ada Lovelace (Ophelia's supposed ancestor), inspired by Fernand Khnopff's nymphs.

Ada was the daughter of the poet Byron, who also had another secret daughter, conceived incestuously with his half-sister. Byron was as famous in his time as Princess Diana was in ours; every era has the stars it deserves. Shortly after Ada's birth, Annabella, the

Romantic dandy's prim wife, who had proven unable to bear her husband's ego and lax morals, demanded a separation and would not allow Byron to see his daughter. She did everything she could to keep the young Ada away from any form of poetry; she was drilled from earliest childhood in self-control and trigonometry.

Raised in the religion of numbers, Ada Lovelace wrote at age twenty-seven what is considered to be the first, embryonic, computer program. Because of this, in the English-speaking countries she has become a hero in the history of feminism (a woman, the 'fore-father' of digital coding!). Ada interested Spielswehk almost as much as her red-headed descendant, and the painter used Ophelia as the model for portraits of her face and body.

Ada died at thirty-six, the same age as her father. Despite her mother's efforts, she had never been stripped of passion; she asked to be buried next to Byron. The relationship between the poet and the austere Annabella, as well as their daughter's fate, enraptured the public during the early Industrial Age. Ada represented a living turning point in history: the conflict between romanticism and reason, poetry and applied science, imagination and the ideology of objective reality.

In 2004, Spielswehk's studio was a colorful jumble of a place overlooking the Parc des Buttes-Chaumont. Other than the canvases and random objects there was very little furniture: a sofa, a low table, and a large four-poster bed. Bardo was unnerved by the bond he sensed between the two women; it seemed like a barrier against him. From the first minute of his visit he felt intimidated and clumsy, and, as if to justify this awkwardness, he fired questions at Ophelia, whose beauty and apparent health didn't fit his idea of what a leukaemia patient should look like.

"Shouldn't you be in a hospital, with your illness?"

Ophelia's only answer was a variation on her usual head-shrug, something between *yes* and *no*.

"What illness?" demanded Spielswehk.

Without a word, Ophelia stood up, grabbed her coat, and walked out. My brother stood up to follow her, but the artist took hold of his arm.

"Leave her alone for a few minutes. I think I know where she's going."

"Do you believe she has leukaemia?"

"She has a vivid imagination."

"But why would she lie?"

"Maybe she's just giving you what you want."

"I want true love."

"Well, yes, of course. But what if it were an ordinary sort of love? You seem like you need passion."

"Just like you. Like a lot of people."

"Not necessarily. Most people run away from passion and great desire. *That we the pain of death would hourly die/Rather than die at once!*"

"Shakespeare. So you think she isn't sick?"

"Ophelia is almost untouchable."

"Almost?"

"She can give herself from time to time. You'll see."

On Spielswehk's advice he found her not far away, in the heights of the Parc des Buttes-Chaumont, sitting at the foot of the belvedere overlooking Paris. The white columns accentuated her anachronistic allure. The shade of Ada Lovelace wasn't far away.

Bardo approached her, feeling the beginnings of vertigo. She was staring at the horizon. He sat down next to her. She didn't move. He took her hand, and she didn't pull away.

Finally she spoke. "I'm supposed to leave tomorrow."

"And go where?"

"Oxford, first, to my dad's house. He's making me try this new treatment in a clinic near New York. They've had success with some types of leukaemia, apparently."

"I'll come and see you."

"No, the hospital's a total mood-killer. I don't want your pity. Anyway, I'm not going."

"Why not?"

"Because I don't believe in miracle cures. Because I don't want to die in a hospital bed."

There was an uneasy silence. My brother felt Ophelia's fingers squeeze his own. She turned and looked closely at him, smiling.

"Can I ask you a question?" she asked. "The day we met, what were you doing at the Place de l'Étoile?"

"Flirting with vertigo at the top of the Arc de Triomphe."

"You like dangerous games?"

"No. Unless . . ."

"Unless what?"

"Unless that's what keeps bringing us together."

"What?"

"That fatal attraction between two beings who don't know whether to be, or not to be."

She didn't answer. Their eyes held the same mixture of innocence and gravity.

Their lips drew closer, and the horizon was suddenly aflame.

15

All the vital seas

Wednesday, August 4th, 2010. I wouldn't necessarily say time has come unhinged, but it is definitely speeding up, as it does when a tragedy is approaching its denouement. It's been two days since I arrived in Tallinn, in the extreme north of continental Europe.

This capital city had the inspiring name of Revel until 1918. I felt touched by it right away; it almost seems to float above the earth. There's something ethereal in the atmosphere here, a light, a feeling of the future and of the past in the breeze that blows through the narrow medieval lanes and flows into the Gulf of Finland. Even the tourists here seem . . . lighter, somehow, at first, but—like tourists everywhere—they would like perhaps to forget, without knowing how to go about it. It would never occur to them, for example, to venture outside the embalmed city center, to where taxis rarely go, among the streets of run-down post-Soviet buildings. It's not difficult, though; all you have to do is what I did, as soon as I got here—just take a bus to its end stop and melt into the urban landscape, telling yourself that you're invisible. Or, even better, that you don't care if anyone can see you or not.

Malnutrition, lethargy, bodies bloated or desiccated by alcohol, sometimes without even the money to buy a pack of cigarettes. Occasionally some drunk brute in a sleeveless top slams his wife's head against a wall. Her lipstick leaves a smeared trace in the dirt, between two security doors, behind which kittens are asleep with their mistress in a flat ten meters square including the kitchen. Mind-numbing American TV shows drone on beneath lines of drying laundry. In more than one lobby, retirees have installed sofas where they vegetate while waiting for something to carry them off. Every once in a while someone checks his mobile phone for messages, just to verify that no one wants anything to do with them.

That same kind of misery punctuated by occasional happy spells is commonplace in other parts of Europe too, including France or Portugal, where my brother and I were born. It transforms grown men into bad-tempered, paranoid children and drama into ritual. It's not all black, but it's far from being rosy either. Bardo and I didn't experience that kind of unhappiness while we were growing up, but in a sense, destiny caught up with us just the same.

This time I've avoided hotels and rented a bare-bones room in an apartment inhabited by Liis, a film student I met on the four-hour bus ride from Riga to Tallinn (her grandmother is Russian but lives in Lithuania). Here, bus seats are numbered and assigned in advance; I hadn't chosen to sit next to the petite blonde with the baby face, neither beautiful nor particularly ugly, but with a frank, honest look. She spoke a little French. Something in her precocious seriousness made me feel like I could open up, and somehow or other in the course of our conversation I ended up telling her everything. She said:

"It's obvious that you have a love of beauty. Love comes before ambition, for me."

"Too much love might kill us all. We'd be paralyzed by a hundred emotions, drown in a thousand desires."

Liis is only twenty-two, but she says she's already experienced true love, with a Spanish guy. She lived with him for a year in Barcelona, but then came to her senses and went back to Estonia.

"My mother never had the chance to be a student. I owe her a degree. That fact has been programmed into me since I was tiny."

She offered to rent me this room for a third of the daily cost of rent, until I find Ophelia. It's cheaper, and more interesting, than a hotel. My window overlooks a run-down courtyard populated by seagulls. The building is dilapidated but beautiful. The room has a mattress and a table, which is all I need anyway. One thing took me by surprise at first; the faucets and locks operate in the opposite direction from what I'm used to. There's a shelf of rare books in the living room, and among them I find a Soviet edition of *Hamlet*.

Bardo never had a good memory. He was fascinated by Ophelia's; she could recite dozens of Shakespearean passages by heart. He did manage to memorize one phrase, though, which he used to quote when he was happy:

> *If music be the food of love, play on, give me*
> *excess of it . . .*

And Bardo played. In the way he knew least badly: poetry. There are far more pages than usual from that time, scribbled by hand, which he read to Ophelia when she asked him to, often late at night. I carry that notebook with me everywhere now.

This evening I've bought some cheese and a nice bottle of French wine to thank my host. Ophelia still hasn't appeared. Maybe she's waiting for us to bump into each other in the street, by chance?

I don't feel very well, despite my efforts. There's a kind of anxiety overwhelming me. Liis asks me to read her a couple of lines of my brother's writing. Whenever I stop, she asks me to continue. Time stands still.

It would be amazing, Ophelia, to analyze the circle of our choices, in the course of our life story.

Thousands of yeses, thousands of noes, and the universal stagnation of shadows behind the elemental doors.

The mechanics of time, with teeth worn down the repetition of everything, the renewal of doubts to the tune of public transport, ambivalence on the corners of the tables.

Sooner or later, the people who don't know how to love you choose to ignore you — or so they believe, but it's in thinking of you that they ignore you.

I believed, like you, that it would be better if everything were forgotten, everything falsified.

I yearned to forget what I wished for; I desired it like ecstasy.

To only go forward.

For a single day to have two hundred and forty hours, stretched out like feelings; for everything incomprehensible to become clear through this slowed development, and for ugliness to be sublimated by the clearness of eyes without expectations.

Your eyes calmed me.

Our bodies claimed each other.

We were two separate people, and yet you rose up like a familiar world, too familiar, perhaps.

It was a race against time, counter-clockwise. Time consists of organic movements, but we couldn't allow one life to pass us by while we waited for another, that love might not be just a foundation on which to build the future, but the very structure of the past.

My days passed sometimes in the darkness of caverns, where I had to double over in order to hold on in the narrowness of the bygone, to beat my head, tear my skin, follow a faint gleam in the distance, and, at first light, not to cry out from thirst I thought I'd forgotten.

I remember a concert, one of our first dates.

A Schumann quintet taunted the threshold of the void, in a secret room in the cellar of a building.

I listened, and battered myself against walls of impatience: why was the trance not total?

Why didn't the music break us down, take us immediately, implacably back?

Why did my resistance, my control, prevent me from turning liquid and evaporating and being lost from sight?

Were we all meant to be satisfied with the insubstantial, mouths hanging open, like near-sighted mastiffs?

Is the effect of sublime things always retroactive, unleashing a slow burn like a sunrise?

I watched your fingers imitate the movements of the pianist's. Were you so touching because I already loved you, or because you had surprised me with the possibility of your death?

After the concert, we roamed the night on our bicycles, searching for our antennae, for a socket to plug our bodies into, and the city lights circled us like a frenzied pack of wolves.

I looked up, and the stars were simple—I felt almost there, almost present. But I knew I was still someone other than me watching, that I was only someone who hoped to be moved, lastingly moved to tears, who hoped to dovetail with the world, simply by naming things.

But it was in vain. Maybe, I told myself, it was a question of language—there is no mother tongue for us, no language that is ours, inner, personal. Singular.

I had a glimpse of a truth, Ophelia: the earth was home only to our doubles, and every human being was represented there by a twin shadow.

The angels, who can no longer tolerate either oxygen or corruption, live elsewhere.

Here, only lies—by omission or remission—were breathable.

Each time we met, it was our common language that I wanted to hear, the gaze of a kindred spirit I wanted to meet, and I let myself be endlessly fooled by similarities: close accents, echoes of words.

When I thought of you, you were my letting-go of purple balloons, the lifeblood of stones, and the present in its totality.

You became my truth. Every note of your soul intoxicated me with its simple evocation. You were the one who would banish illusion.

Your eyes were honest, where so many people's weren't. When I thought back to conversations with them, I remembered the note of perdition in their eyes.

Sometimes, Ophelia, I would see a piece of rusted metal and it looked resistant to me, like an old soul that had managed, somehow, to stay alive.

And then, one day I was that old soul, and I felt my skin stretch like a child's, until my features became smooth, like a mirror.

Sometimes I would stand at the center of an intersection, waiting for the arrows of truth, before realizing that the place was changing every second—that the arrows were passing me by without hitting me. The dimensions changed with every shift of the time-beat. Life was an octopus with rhythmic tentacles, ad-

vancing slowly, producing images with each breath.

We are metamorphic, you and I. We only appear in human form to caress one another's cheek, or when you whisper in my ear that the hard helmets of the days could be decorated with flowers, and that the soldiers of destiny don't always come to kill.

Our destiny is truly glorious, Ophelia, and it will triumph in strange ways.

It's up to me, now, to live like an axis, where before I was only a rattle. I used to have pockets overstuffed with marbles; they spilled out and fell, and that abundance seemed fatal to me—it was a game. No one knows what a heart can do.

Yesterday I picked up a box of matches and shook it.

I listened, and I was surprised. It was as if straw foetuses were fighting in the box, though no single match could escape from the rhythm I was imposing on them, because of the box. Maybe each of them dreamed of bursting into flame.

To wait, or not to wait.

Come, shadows of the past, and buy me an ice cream—which I will allow to melt while I remember the summers I spent almost alone, always fighting, far from you, among the matches.

To burn, or not to burn.

I've reached my tipping point, a development beyond substance, the first name of a *suicidal girl who must either save me or finish me off, so that I can be reborn.*

We are the children of the irrepressible.

You, passing through gilded serpents, a dreamlike statue, emanation of a mad desire, and my nation.

I saw too much sadness in the silence of others. Never run away from love, because that would be the nihilism of a tree: not producing leaves in the spring because they will die in the autumn. Time changes shapes and colors.

Some have woven a fabric from these that must be endlessly resewn.

Others have traded them for sleep, and so their nights are restless, believing, and then not believing anymore.

With you, I will no longer be sitting in one place, wondering what to do—a separation, a reversal of the situation, an estrangement, the invention of the present.

Because we have opened up space and time.

And out of our ruins, we have built a bridge over this river that flows through all the vital seas.

16

Imminent danger

I feel like time is getting faster every day now, that space is shrinking, that my words are getting closer and closer to the event.

Yesterday morning, August 8th, 2010, the spirit-boy appeared to me.

I'd just spent a restless night tossing and turning in bed. Coffee didn't make me feel any better. I felt incapable of writing—a voice inside me kept murmuring that everything was in vain, because Bardo was dead. It was like a cold hand was gripping, squeezing, my heart.

I was standing at the window of my room, projecting wishes—if not for news of Ophelia, then at least to be able to tell what, out of love for Bardo, hadn't yet been brought to light. The apartment was quiet; Liis must still have been sleeping, or maybe she'd spent the night at her boyfriend's. I stared at the windows across from mine, but no human form detached itself from them to tell another story. As a child, I often imagined, with a hint of melancholy, the living lines sketching themselves behind the opaque openings of buildings.

Would I ever feel at home again, anywhere?

I guess I've probably given you an overly idealized image of my brother up to now. For me he was pretty close to perfect, except that he had trouble making choices when he thought the alternative was useless, and making those decisions which for him didn't have to do with anything deeply significant. And he wasn't much good at participating in the codes and rituals of social interaction—there, again, I feel I am just stacking up dead formulas. Since his death, I've polished and honed sentences with a focus that is undoubtedly serving to contain my rage. The near future frightens me.

Liis says that time is our enemy, and that life is unfair. I don't want to prove her right.

For several days now I've been having episodes of déjà-vu. Does this mean that destiny is finally showing its face?

So I was there in my room, turning these feelings of almost-madness over and over in my head, when I heard a clear little voice, right next to me:

"I'm the one that called you."

I saw him, and he was beautiful. The spitting image of my brother as a little boy.

He was sitting on the bed, humble and touching. His gaze was determined.

"You do look like him," he said. "But not really. I'm the one who sent you the text signed with Ophelia's name."

"So you can communicate in normal ways too?"

"She doesn't like it much when I teleport. She's afraid to see you."

"You can teleport?"

94

"Well . . . not really. I can project myself. It started when I began wondering who my father was."

"But why Tallinn?"

"I don't think she even knows, herself. She's always running further north. She's terrified, you know."

"I figured as much. You should let me protect you both. Where are you staying?"

"Near the harbor. In a kind of hostel. It's always full of people. Sometimes we take a walk to the Maar-jamäe Memorial, which overlooks Tallinn Bay. It's pretty there. We look at the horizon and watch the boats leaving."

"Where is it?"

"In the north-eastern part of the city. It's a big prom-ontory, with a stone spur jutting out of it. There's a cemetery next to it. You'll be able to talk to her there."

"Today?"

"Soon. It's not quite time yet. You haven't told the whole story."

And he was gone.

✳

Nervous, I get dressed to go out. I decide to go to the Maarjamäe Memorial. It's at least an hour's walk from the city center, an ominous, eloquent place, with a tall obelisk that's meant to look like a blade. There's no one around. The sea is on one side of me, a little wooded area on the other, and above me the clouds seem to be trying to fill the sky, puffing up with tears, desire, emptiness.

Right at this very moment, I know that I can never go back, that the tick-tock of the clock is getting louder, like fingernails scratching rhythmically at the bark that separates us from life.

Is the poet's death calling for more blood?

I take a photo of the obelisk with my phone. It seems like an omen.

This monument to emptiness started out as a piece of propaganda, built for the Soviet Olympic Games in 1980, which were as boycotted as the Nazi's Berlin Games in 1936. Now the Maarjamäe Memorial is dedicated to the Second World War. Just a few meters away from that is a cemetery where both Russian soldiers and German war dead are buried, the two sides commingling in death.

It's an apocalyptic landscape.

Bardo would have found it sublime. I think I understand why he talked sometimes about being finished with *Homo sapiens*; it's a species that, behind its bland airs, is being eaten away at by a drunken desire for destruction, a passion for horror.

Two kilometers from here, behind the woods are post-Soviet apartment buildings, blocks of pastel concrete as far as the eye can see, inhabited by Russian-speakers, mostly. Monuments to boredom and the persistence of class society.

I stay here for two hours, like a sentinel.

Ophelia doesn't appear.

Even so, I feel a sense of imminent danger.

17

Do you want to meet my father?

By the summer of 2004, Ophelia felt as if she were falling deeper and deeper in love with Bardo, just as he was putting—or at least he thought so—a safer distance between them. Their love wasn't without its problems; she often avoided any physical contact with him in public, and most of the time she would only let him kiss her when they were alone in a room together. Even in private, she wasn't always able to let herself go. She complained that my brother was too sensual; it was excessive, she said, and went against the sublimation of the flesh. But sometimes she seemed to go almost crazy with desire, and then he was the one who had trouble dealing with her ardor. He thought this unbalanced state of things must have been caused by something in her past, but she remained vague on the subject. This resulted in a series of misunderstandings, made worse by the fact that Bardo was always expecting a new lie, even though she really seemed to be making an effort to be truthful with him.

One evening they attended a five-hour-long performance of Wagner's *Tristan and Isolde* at the Opéra Bastille. Ophelia cried at the end of Act One, but then froze up completely during Acts Two and Three. She had felt something like a sharp burning sensation, something premonitory in the irrational love between the legendary couple, a liaison allowed only because they had first decided to die. That intensity reminded her that she would have, perhaps, preferred a simpler life.

And she felt—she knew—that Bardo's gaze wasn't quite as admiring any more when he looked at her, that he had become wary after she admitted to him that she didn't have leukaemia.

She was still staying in Spielswehk's studio, where she assisted the artist while doing a bit of painting herself. It hadn't taken Bardo long to realize that the two women sometimes shared a bed. One evening, two weeks after she first arrived, Ophelia—who had spent the afternoon lugging around heavy objects—had had a painful backache. Spielswehk hadn't stopped looking at her. A massage took care of the rest. It was a totally new experience for Ophelia, to feel her own body capable of abandoning itself completely to pleasure, far from any threatening masculinity.

A bizarre triangle was formed that summer: Spielswehk restored to Ophelia's body the suppleness and sensuality it had been missing, and Ophelia in turn was able to share Bardo's simple desire with a bit less reticence. He tried his best to adapt to the situation; a poet, after all, should be open-minded. He could deal with a few hours of solitude. A lone wolf, he reminded himself proudly, can never bear to be with people for too long, even the ones he loves.

The weeks passed fairly pleasantly, entropically. One autumn evening, after they had dined in Spielswehk's studio while the leaves fell outside, the artist had proposed a game of Scrabble. It might have been the incongruity of the situation, or the Spanish red wine, but the party became a really joyous one, and even held a moment of revelation for Bardo, when he played the six-letter word *chance*.

He had never stopped believing in the power of words. Dazzled by epiphany, he suddenly saw everything good that had ever happened to him in the past as having been caused by chance. He would have to learn—even more—to let go, to clutch less desperately at the rudder of will. To trust the wind, and put the importance of his destination ports into perspective.

That night, he took Ophelia back to his place. In the wee hours, while she slept beside him, he lay awake, turning the idea of chance over and over in his mind. He got up and, still trusting in the power of words, opened the dictionary to a random page. He closed his eyes, pressed a finger down, and saw with surprise that he had landed on the word *harass*. Next, he picked a stranger's name out of the phone book. He dialed the number, was greeted by a woman's sleepy voice, and hung up without daring to say anything.

"Who are you calling in the middle of the night?"

It was Ophelia's voice behind him. He turned around, his expression that of a guilty child.

"A woman . . . but I don't know her . . ." he babbled.

"Oh, well, that's reassuring. What did you want with her?"

"Uh . . . to harass her?"

She gave a snort of laughter. "Good to know I'm not the only one who's capable of acting ridiculous. Someday I'll tell you what it's really like to be harassed, and not by a stranger."

"Tell me now."

"You're a poet, aren't you? So you have to see and understand for yourself."

Needless to say, Bardo immediately abandoned the idea of submitting someone to constant unwanted little attacks and annoying actions, including threats and demands (which is the technical definition of harassment). But he still couldn't stop playing the game of chance that his mind—worn down by his relationship with Ophelia—had created in an attempt to learn to be more open-minded—and to distract himself from the slight sense of inferiority he felt around Spielswehk.

Whenever the atmosphere becomes too heavy, the poet instinctively turns into a clown. The next evening he headed, alone, for a bowling alley located not far from the Tour Montparnasse. *Bowling*, you see, was the word he'd just chosen at random from the office dictionary. It seemed kind of appropriate; after all, he'd been feeling, these last few months, about as welcome as a dog in a game of skittles.

So it was that he found himself wearing a pair of multi-colored shoes and throwing a series of wobbly gutter-balls, wondering what the hell he was even doing there. In the lane next to his, two massive, drunken teenagers took turns doing dangerously exaggerated imitations of each other's clumsiness. The stronger of the two misguidedly flung his ball to the left—and it crashed down on Bardo's head.

My brother was knocked out cold.

He woke up in the hospital with an impressive lump on his head and one hell of a headache, but no other serious aftereffects.

Ophelia was sitting next to his white-blanketed bed.

"What in the world possessed you? That's the stupidest accident I've ever—"

"We're children of chance, Ophelia."

"You've been pretty childish lately, I'll give you that."

"Ophelia, I love you. Which means that I would die for you. But you have to be less distant. I need to know what's eating away at you."

She looked at the bandage covering my brother's head and took a deep breath.

"Do you want to meet my father?"

18

Disappearing into the night

He'd loved her wholeheartedly again, he thought, since waking up in that hospital bed, opening his eyes and seeing her face with its look of maternal tenderness. Soon they would leave for England and he would experience Ophelia's homeland, so close to Stratford-upon-Avon and that whole Shakespearean world in which she'd grown up.

Ophelia hadn't seen her father in almost a year, and she seemed extremely nervous—but she comforted herself with the thought that she was also going to see William again. During the journey she often looked deep into my brother's eyes. I realize now that she must have hoped that some kind of miracle would come out of that trip. Something like a transfer of power. She thought Bardo was strong enough to face down the dragon without losing his nerve—to change the order of things without having his wings clipped in the process. Did she know the kind of risk she was asking him to take?

They took a train to London and then a bus into the English countryside. A fine, misty rain was falling that evening. The family home stood a few kilometers outside the center of Oxford, in the village of Stanton St. John. It was a stone cottage with white-framed windows in the middle of an orderly garden—but behind its chocolate-box prettiness there was a strange sense of power, dominated by a church that looked like a fortified castle.

Peter Lovelace was regarded in Oxford as an expert on Shakespeare, a professorial authority and distant descendant of Byron. His students either loved or hated him—but most of all they feared this dry, erudite man who walked with a stiff gait and flew into rages that had become legendary on the university campus. The students had long ago given him the ironic nickname of 'Loveface'.

At first, he received the couple with more surprise than coldness, even seeming tired, like a man who had given up tormenting his daughter. It would be terrible to think—but it's not outside the realm of possibility— that Bardo, involuntarily, reawakened his jealousy and treachery somehow. On the train, Ophelia had tried to warn my brother:

"Don't tell him you're a poet. He won't understand that. Just say you're an architect; that'll be okay."

On that first evening Bardo took the father's lack of talkativeness to mean that he had spent time thinking about what he had done. He didn't seem particularly harsh with his daughter, but he wasn't soft with her either. Two or three times, with no real cause, his eyes filled with tears.

William, though considered 'abnormal', had had a more spontaneous reaction; they hadn't heard from Ophelia since the previous winter, and her sudden reappearance sent the teenager into raptures, complete with expressive exclamations of joy. He paced the living room, wringing his hands as if to get rid of excess electricity, and then attached himself to Ophelia like a lap dog, the soul of a child trapped in the body of a hulking adolescent.

On the day after their arrival she decided to make lunch, assisted by a still-euphoric William, while Bardo explored the library with its collection of precious volumes, none of which was more recent than Byron. Literature, for Peter Lovelace, had clearly stopped in 1820.

The professor returned from his classes at around one o'clock in the afternoon. Their conversation around the lunch table was awkward at first, with the father making a visible effort to exert himself. He interrogated Bardo in alternating French and English:

"Ophelia tells me you're an architect? Very impressive."

"Yes, part-time."

"Part-time? How strange! And what do you do the rest of the time?"

"It isn't important, Father," Ophelia interjected.

"So, young man, you spend half your time doing things that aren't important?"

"You might say that."

"And what kind of things, if it isn't a mystery? It's not my daughter who's taking up so much of your time, I hope."

"It *is* a mystery. I write poems."

Peter Lovelace let his knife clatter to the table. His whole body stiffened. Suddenly he no longer seemed like an elderly man, but an enraged military commander. He kept his eyes on Ophelia as he spoke:

"A poet?"

"A poet, if it's possible," put in Bardo.

"It isn't possible."

"Why not?"

"Because Shakespeare is a poet! And your Racine. And Ovid, and a few others—they were poets. And no one else! Without tragedy and a superior mind, there is no poetry. I see confused little runts all around me every day who insist they're seers. They're like flies; they only want to play their little buzzing games. No one who isn't a geometrician should ever claim to be a poet."

Bardo paused for a beat, then:

"And your ancestor, Byron?"

"He was . . . a demi-poet, let's say. It was no accident that Byron died in Greece—and the last traces of a dying civilization with him, no doubt. Poetry was buried along with overwrought romanticism and the end of virtue."

"So, poetry is a moral affair, then?"

"I'm not talking about sanctimoniousness. I'm talking about virile courage."

"Ah, because I thought it was certain exegetes—like yourself—who were responsible for the death of poetry, with your endless explaining of texts and lack of imagination."

Peter Lovelace, without responding, looked at Ophelia, his eyes filled with a kind of threatening entreaty. She lowered her head, confused. He had taken on that cutting, judgmental air again, the one she knew all too well. He changed the subject, probably to indicate his contempt for Bardo.

"Have you visited your mother's grave in Paris?"

"Yes, Father."

"Your mother was crazy. It was the French side of her."

William let out a persistent groan that sounded mournful and began rocking his head back and forth. Bardo felt he had to speak up:

"I don't think the French are that crazy, actually."

"Monsieur, *these times of woe afford no time to woo.*"

"Shakespeare. *Romeo and Juliet.*"

"Ah, so you're not completely ignorant."

After a long moment of silence, my brother decided to lighten the atmosphere by bringing up the biography of Shakespeare he'd read just before meeting Ophelia for the first time. When he mentioned the rumor that the first version of *Romeo and Juliet* had been censored by the Church, a spark of interest flared in the professor's eyes, and his face lit up.

"I know that myth. The first thing you should know is that Shakespeare didn't care very much about writing manuscripts. We have almost nothing in his own hand. His plays were re-transcribed by friends, often actors in his troupe. So it's risky to talk about the first version of a play."

"The legend talks about looking another person in the eyes . . ."

"Yes. I remember seeing an old book in the university library that alluded to that."

Lovelace stood up, and added:

"If you like, you can try to find that mysterious phrase tomorrow. Spending some time with Shakespeare will do you good."

"Will you help us, Father?" asked Ophelia, looking up.

He hesitated. "We'll see. My opinion is that this supposed censorship is a literary myth."

Bardo was impressed by the magnificence of Oxford. The Bodleian Library was located in the Tower of the Five Orders, a fortress surrounded by motley columns. A slip of paper signed by Pr. Lovelace gained them entry to the vast Shakespearean section, proud preserver and digitizer of several folios, some of which were almost four hundred years old.

After a few moments, thanks to the father's directions, the couple unearthed a seventeenth-century volume. Ophelia deciphered the index: there was a small subsection of one chapter referring to the censored line spoken by Friar Laurence to Romeo and Juliet during their marriage ceremony.

Whether true or an invention of literary history, the missing passage was re-transcribed here in full:

> *If ever thou wast thyselves, and overcomst by sad*
> *With cloak of dank depression thyselves clad*
> *When death is lulled with masks and merry hours*
> *Seek yon love, grace not the rot of flowers*
> *But take regard and stop not til is past*
> *Time eight hundred eighty-eight breaths should last*
> *Thus comes in view the way that way shall be*
> *For lovers such, full well their destiny*

"It seems like a long time, eight hundred and eighty-eight breaths," observed Ophelia once they were outside, on the university's large green.

"That's counting one inhalation or exhalation every four seconds. It would take about an hour."

"I don't think it would be possible to look into someone else's eyes for that long."

They stopped, and their eyes met. Bardo's face was serious.

"I don't like how your father treats you."

"We'll leave. It was a bad idea to come here."

"What's the story between you?"

"I'll tell you when we're back in Paris."

"Will you really?"

"I'll try."

At dinner that evening, a new crisis exploded when Peter Lovelace asked the couple, with marked irony, if they planned to marry—adding that *Romeo and Juliet* seemed to advise that it might be better never to wed.

"It's clear, Monsieur Bardo, that you've managed to make my daughter fall in love with you, despite your ridiculous nickname. That in itself indicates a lack of taste. You should also know that no poet has been tolerated in the Lovelace family since George Gordon Byron. We might not be as strict as Ada Lovelace's mother—we recognize fields other than mathematics, for example: law, architecture, I suppose; even professorship. But poetry can be nothing more than a degenerate activity." He smiled ambivalently. "I won't have any *vers*"—using the French word for *worms*—"in the fruit."

Ophelia looked at Bardo, who judged it better not to answer these provocative remarks. She, on the other hand, spoke up with some heat:

"And following the funeral processions of strangers to Père-Lachaise, is that degenerate too? Because I've done that two or three times since moving to Paris, Father. I wanted to get an idea of what it was like to attend a person's funeral—to watch them being buried—instead of having them just disappear, like magic."

Peter Lovelace turned to Bardo with a look of false innocence on his face.

"She always has to bring that up, you see. I wanted to protect her. She was only ten. I don't think I could have borne it, to see her next to her mother's coffin. It would have broken my heart."

Ophelia's voice was icy. "You don't have a heart. You lied to me for weeks after she died, telling me that she might come back. I thought she'd abandoned us."

"She did. She was weak."

"Because she could handle the fact that you touched me, that you came to my bed!"

"You're as crazy as your mother was. You want your little bard to believe that you have an incestuous father? If there's a victim in this whole business, it's me. I could have been legendary, like so many other Lovelaces. I could have written a great work of literature! Marriage and women are a death sentence for ambition. Your mother killed herself because she wanted to make me feel guilty for the rest of my life."

"You could even have been a great poet," my brother put in, his voice dripping with sarcasm.

Ophelia turned to Bardo, her eyes full of tears. Peter Lovelace seized a knife, clenching the handle in his fist.

"Get out, both of you," he snarled, "or I'll kill you!"

William, who up to this point had been sitting silently across from his father, seemingly lost in his own misery, now grabbed a knife as well, chanting: "Kill! Kill! Kill! Kill!"

An hour later, the couple was in a taxi, heading out of Stanton St. John and bound for France. Bardo, holding Ophelia tightly to him, looked out the window at the village church disappearing into the night.

19

She wanted to protect him

On the train home, Ophelia withdrew into a cocoon of silence from which she emerged only to offer brief, infrequent responses. Bardo didn't push her; he treated her gently and tried to gather his own thoughts. The claim of incest horrified him. Was it just another lie?

He had always been bored by normal girls, but in fleeing them he'd found a flower on the edge of a cliff, a rose hidden away among brambles.

In the days following their return, Ophelia shut herself away in her room at Spielswehk's house and refused to see him.

He wrote to her. She didn't answer. This little game lasted a week, during which my brother, powerless in the face of her silence, was tempted to fall into a rage. Finally, she called him and suggested a walk in the Parc de Saint-Cloud.

He met her not far from his house, at the very western edge of the park, near a carefully-upkept rustic farm complete with several grazing sheep. There was also a white horse, which from a distance looked like a unicorn. His heart swelled in his chest when he saw Ophelia coming, a feminine exclamation point that caused wages of mingled compassion, admiration, and desire. She wore a skirt short enough to make her observers feel a bit warm, if not her legs.

"I've missed you," he murmured.

She didn't answer, just made that habitual childish gesture with her head, somewhere between 'yes' and 'no'.

It was a Thursday morning, 14 October 2004. They walked in silence along the almost-empty paths, shadowed by the enormous trees. They held hands. They felt lighter and lighter, the further they went into the deserted park. They stretched out on the grass. They kissed. They even made love, in the shade of a hedge.

That was surely the day you were conceived, Bernardo.

Afterward, she showed him her arm—or rather, she arranged herself so that he would see it: like a teenager, she had written with a pen on her wrist, right in the place where suicides cut their veins: *I love Bardo.*

When he saw the inscription, my brother's good mood evaporated.

She had to write it down so she'd remember it, he thought, *like a telephone number. Her mood is too changeable. She only loves me some of the time . . . or maybe the trip to London ruined everything.*

He got up. Something in him had turned to steel. He felt a vague sense of disgust rising in his chest; smiled to hide his confusion.

"I'm cold," she said. "We won't have to see each other again for a few weeks."

"I don't even know if that's the truth anymore."

"What?"

"That you're cold. Or hot. I don't feel like I can fully trust anything you say you feel."

She frowned and rose, dignified. "Anyway, I'm going back to Oxford."

"How can you go back to live with that man, if he's as evil as you say?"

"That man is my father. William needs me. And I don't want to feel hunted anymore."

"Then I'll come with you."

"No, that would be worse. I'm going to try to smooth things over, but it'll take time. I'm coming back. I need to confront my father once and for all. Otherwise he'll never leave me in peace."

They walked side by side for another few meters, and then she stopped.

"I'm leaving in a week."

"That's ridiculous. I forbid you to go."

"Only my father can forbid me to do things."

They parted on the Saint-Cloud bridge, without a kiss goodbye.

Bardo walked back through the park on foot, stunned at finding himself suddenly so alone. Barely an hour earlier, he had thought he was happy.

Three days of hostile silence followed. She didn't answer any of his messages.

On October 18th, 2004, Bardo, defeated, decided to go and celebrate his newfound solitude at the top of the Arc de Triomphe.

Seven months had passed since he had dodged traffic in his pursuit of Ophelia. From up here the view of Paris seemed unchanged, as if indifferent to the twists and turns, the joys and suffering woven through the lives of its inhabitants. He approached the edge of the imposing belvedere. As usual, he looked down, and was seized by vertigo.

He breathed, silently.

He felt terrible. Worse than usual. He dreaded the weeks to come. The breeze caressed his face. He gripped the metal bars protecting him with both hands and leaned further and further forward.

He thought he heard Ophelia's voice:

"Could you do it?"

He turned his head. It was no apparition. She was standing beside him.

This time, their encounter had nothing to do with chance. He'd told her about his ritual; she'd known that she had a good chance of finding him on this platform on a Sunday evening. She'd come for him.

He smiled.

"So you're staying?"

She made that catlike movement with her head. Without saying a word she leaned out next to him, a few centimeters from the void.

"No," she said at last. "I have to confront him. I don't see any other outcome. Unless . . ."

Bardo looked deeply into her eyes, and was surprised. It occurred to him that—could it be?—she was suggesting that they jump together. The idea was intoxicating. Taking her with him into death might be a victory—perhaps the only imaginable triumph.

He drew himself up. She did likewise. Their shoulders touched, as they had done in the metro carriage that had taken them to the République station. For once, he was in control of the situation. There were few other visitors at this time of the evening, but they would have to act fast, before they drew too much attention to themselves.

They looked at each other. They were thinking of the same thing: the temptation to be done with it all. Together.

In just a few seconds they had stepped over the low safety bars without being seen. Both of them felt nearly ready to leap together into the air. It was an exhilarating sensation, like hovering above the world.

Then, suddenly, they both had the same feeling in the pit of the stomach, as if a cold hand were gripping, tearing at their hearts. They gasped for breath. Ophelia's foot slipped. She felt herself losing her balance.

Bardo pulled her back, clinging to the metal bars. They looked away from the ground far below them, to gaze into each other's eyes.

Neither of them needed to speak, to understand that they had both just thought of the same thing: eight hundred and eighty-eight breaths. They began to count out loud, there on the edge of the void, eye in eye, hand in hand, their faces crossed by smiles and then shadows.

Seventeen, eighteen, nineteen. They counted each inhalation and exhalation. Their breaths fell into perfect sync. The vertigo seemed to dissipate.

"You can't stay up here," a voice interrupted them.

It was a security guard. They were quickly ushered downstairs and out of the monument.

Three days later, Ophelia left for London.

One month after that, she fled to Hamburg, sending Bardo only one brief text message: "I don't know why, but he hates you even more than the others. He's stronger than I am."

For five years, she refused to see my brother. In her rare responses, she insisted that she didn't love him anymore. She wanted to protect him.

20

I am Bardo

Life isn't a novel. You can't correct the present, or edit it. You can only take refuge behind a screen, *a posteriori*, and use logic to connect each of your actions to the preceding one. It was written that August 14th, 2010 would be fixed, in a few moments and in a most unusual way, as the denouement of this tragedy.

It was quick, and surreal in appearance, like everything that slices into this collective hallucination we call everyday life.

On that day, a rumor floated around Tallinn.

They said it was better not to go out. A radioactive cloud was passing over the city. Because of the heatwave, peat bogs had been on fire for three days just a few kilometers outside Chernobyl in Ukraine, site of the worst nuclear catastrophe in human history. As contaminated areas burned, the fires released radioactive nuclides present in the soil and humus into the air. Wind and rain then spread these radioactive substances over hundreds of kilometers. It was that day that Ophelia chose to meet me on the promontory of the Maarjamäe Memorial.

I hadn't seen her for more than five years. My

brother had been dead for three months, and the bitterness that I had felt toward her, who I felt to be the indirect cause of all this drama, had—at least partially—dispersed into the gulf of Finland. I felt responsible for little Bernardo; as my brother had asked me to, I had to take care of this little five-year-old stranger and of his mother, whatever it cost me.

I walked along the quayside through a misty—and probably radioactive—rain. In my pocket was the wooden kaleidoscope that Bardo never had the chance to give to his son.

It couldn't have taken me more than thirty or forty minutes to reach the memorial. The sky had cleared, just a bit. I walked up the long concrete ramp that led to the center of the monument. I was alone. Reaching the foot of the giant stone sword, I felt the same sense of grandiose desolation as I had when I explored the place for the first time a week earlier.

It was nine o'clock at night, and I waited. The sun, in all its ruddy twilit beauty, was sinking behind the bay of Tallinn.

Like an echo of the solar disk, Ophelia appeared.

Long-limbed and slender, holding the mysterious Bernardo by the hand. As I watched her approach I thought I understood what my brother had felt for her: a mixture of compassion and admiration. When they were ten meters or so away from me, it occurred to me that the child, his face impassive, had an aura like that of the gods.

She extended her hand, visibly uncomfortable. Her eyes moved to Bernardo:

"You two have already met, I believe."

Bernardo remained silent, but his intense gaze

plunged into my own. He was the same here as when his spirit had appeared to me; in fact, tonight he seemed even more ethereal, though clearly made of flesh and bone. I felt an intense desire to know him better, and to love him. To feel his existence as a simple child, to watch him play, learn, and grow solid with time, instead of having this unreal quality. He looked so much like the Bardo I had known thirty years ago.

I felt awkward, like I used to when I compared myself to my brother. I said to Ophelia:

"Why did you want to meet here?"

"Bernardo really likes this place. He loves to wander among the soldiers' tombs."

In the distance, off to the left, you could see the outlines of the ancient buildings in the historic center of Tallinn. I was about to suggest that we walk there before it got completely dark, when Ophelia looked over my shoulder and let out a cry:

"William!"

I turned around and saw a burly figure walking toward us, alone in the middle of the tree-encircled stone boulevard. Instantly I recognized the silhouette of the football fan on Inspector Kreiss's surveillance video.

William was carrying something in his hands, something that seemed to embarrass him. Behind him, emerging from the top of the ramp, came a rigid silhouette with a measured step: Peter Lovelace.

As they drew near to us, I saw that William held a revolver.

Peter Lovelace's face was suffused with sarcasm. "I hate traveling. Hamburg and Tallinn in one year—it'll kill me."

I turned toward Ophelia, angry. "Did you tell him we'd be here?"

The professor scrutinized me. "Bally hell, you really do look just like him. William's going to have to kill the same man twice."

He patted the head of little Bernardo, who remained unmoved, preserving his imposing silence. Lovelace quickly withdrew his hand.

"It's thanks to this little fellow that we're here. He's a very good guide, with unique methods. He'd appear and tell you to be somewhere, and a few days later somewhere else. Without him, I'd never have been able to trace Ophelia to Hamburg."

I looked at the child, horrified. Ophelia shook her head, her eyes full of tears. Bernardo gazed at us calmly. He spoke then, in a voice that was assured and eloquent far beyond his years:

"There are some things you will never see on a surveillance camera. I was there during the sacrifice at the Sternschanze metro station. William didn't throw him completely off-balance, but Bardo had to die. So he could be reborn. At the last second, with a word, I encouraged him to fall. He'd been anticipating that drop for a long time."

So it was the son who had killed his father.

"Why?" I screamed.

The child—was it really a child?—remained eerily calm:

"So he could come back. Stronger. Soon."

William didn't fully understand what was happening. He was fiddling dangerously with the gun. Peter Lovelace wrenched it from his hands.

"There's been quite enough of this chaos."

Bardo looked at him.

"You are weak."

"Is that what you see?"

"Only weaklings need weapons of technology. An Überpoet uses only his mind."

"A what?" the professor asked impatiently. "Ophelia, we're going home. Say goodbye to the poet's double and to your degenerate son."

I exploded with fury and stupefaction. "You're insane!"

"True men fight an equal match, Grandfather," the boy persisted, still perfectly serene. "You have a choice of weapons."

"But I already *have* a weapon, you little ignoramus! He's more deranged than his father."

"Then let me choose the weapons."

Peter Lovelace barked out a laugh. "And what would those weapons be? Your little fists?"

"Eyes."

"Eyes?"

"I propose a duel. Lasting for eight hundred and eighty-eight breaths."

"Balderdash! Shakespeare never wrote that."

"Then there is nothing to fear. There will still be time to kill us afterward."

"But what you're proposing is extremely tedious, child."

"If you have a sense of honor, you'll accept."

"Ah, trying to buy time, are we? Think you're one of the chosen people who can do anything with one look? As long as I'm alive, children will honor their fathers. William, hold on to this gun. If they try to take it, or to run away, you shoot. But do not shoot your sister, do you hear me?"

The teenager gave an amused snort. "Kill!"

So this was the bizarre scene to which Ophelia and I were witness: the child and his grandfather sitting cross-legged at the edge of the promontory, above the road and the sea, face to face. The sky still held fiery tints. In an hour it would be dark. The little boy asked me to count their breaths aloud, with one breath around every four seconds. He added:

"If one of us looks away, the other gets the gun, and can do whatever he wants with it. All right?"

Peter Lovelace knew there was no turning back. "I'm ready," he said, with dignity.

Bernardo gave me the signal to start. He fixed his neutral gaze on Peter Lovelace's, which was hostile. I began to count.

"One . . . two . . . three . . ."

They seemed equally imperturbable, equally determined. I trembled as I counted.

"Thirty-three, thirty-four . . ."

They stared unwaveringly at each other.

Peter Lovelace seemed to have the upper hand, if only because he was looking down at the child from above.

"Fifty-five, fifty-six . . ."

It was like they had never seen one another before.

"Eighty-eight, eighty-nine, ninety . . ."

Each of them was assailed by images from the past; familiar faces and friendly ones, monstrous and frozen ones.

They felt their heartbeats slowing down slightly.

"One hundred and twenty, one hundred and twenty-one . . ."

They weren't seeing each other's eyes anymore, but rather something like the fusion of dozens, hundreds of perspectives above the memorial.

They could sense the worlds contained in each other's souls, and Lovelace's resembled a devastated battlefield.

"Two hundred and fifty-three, two hundred and fifty-four . . ."

They felt as if they were becoming each other, beginning to know everything about each other. Peter Lovelace had tears in his eyes and sweat on his forehead, but his gaze remained steady. Bernardo, however, seemed to be wavering a bit. He seemed to be frightened by what he was seeing. He seemed ready to cry out.

But he managed to hold on. Ophelia gripped my hand, breathing with difficulty. Occasionally she darted a glance at William and gestured for him to give her the gun—but each time her brother would take a step backward. He seemed dazed, desolate. Lost.

"Three hundred and six, three hundred and seven . . ."

The boy and his grandfather no longer knew where they were.

They no longer knew whether they were surrounded by people, or souls.

Or parts of the same soul.

"Four hundred and eighty-two, four hundred and eighty-three . . ."

It seemed to them that they were shifting through all the forms of life, gradually. That they were old men and then newborn babies, trees and then tombs, the roots and the air and the stone of the promontory.

"Five hundred, five hundred and one . . ."

A fiery whirlwind swept over their burning bodies.

Peter Lovelace's face grew more and more contorted.

I saw a single tear trickle down the little boy's cheek.

"Six hundred and forty-four, six hundred and forty-five . . ."

They felt themselves becoming like seawater. In that water, the bloody bodies of sirens floated. The professor's face was crimson. Their eyes remained locked.

"Seven hundred and seventy-six, seven hundred and seventy-seven . . ."

None of my clumsy words could do justice to their state of mind after that. I believe the child's soul and his grandfather's became one, like when a couple infinitely in love is united.

"Eight hundred and eighty-six, eight hundred and eighty-seven . . ."

Peter Lovelace gave a stifled cry.

His head fell forward.

His body was still.

Bernardo straightened, as if in a trance, and murmured:

"My name is Bardo."

Ophelia leapt toward her son and took him in her arms, weeping. William threw the gun to the ground the way you would fling away a burning object and joined their embrace, giving inhuman cries. I seized the revolver.

The child drew back, slowly. He looked at me, smiling. He was radiant with joy.

"I am the poet reincarnated. I am Bardo."

21

As if in a dream

The ambulance reached the Maarjamäe Memorial at around eleven o'clock that night, shortly after our call. Death was noted at the scene. Officially, Peter Lovelace had died of cardiac arrest while on holiday, having come to meet his beloved daughter in Estonia.

Before leaving the promontory, I lifted my eyes to the sky. A few stars were beginning to twinkle. William was weeping in his sister's arms. My gaze came to rest on the point of the vast stone sword. Little Bardo came up to me, and asked if I had the kaleidoscope. Still in shock, I took it out of my pocket and, as if sleepwalking, handed it to him.

He dug a hole and buried it at the foot of the monument.

"It isn't a sword anymore," he said. "It's an obelisk now. The most valued kind of pillar."

I'm writing these last few lines on August 28th, 2010. I've temporarily moved with the child, Ophelia, and William into the cottage in Stanton St. John, which she inherited. The place is beautiful, with its green fields and woods. My brother was right; the church does look like a fortified castle. For the first time in a long time I can say that I feel happy—though it's going to take some time, yet, to understand what has happened to me.

Ophelia has showed me a piece of my brother's writing that I'd never read. It's from the beginning of May. I've reproduced it here, in full:

> *I've wandered for twenty centuries in the desert, through the tempest.*
>
> *I flowed like lava beneath forests.*
>
> *I pushed reality beyond its limits and everything, even walls, washed through me; sustenance was rare at times.*
>
> *Silken threads bound the atmosphere, shining like filaments, persistent as a passing fancy.*
>
> *I look at my hands; they seem to be independent of me: I breathe on them and it is the warm Vent du Midi. On one hand I disappear, and on the other I am reborn as many, clothed in ever-changing skins.*
>
> *Time enjoys echoes of ecstasies, fleshly threads plunged beneath the earth to rise again later in a state of magnetization.*
>
> *The time of greatest value has come; it is the time of the Worldforming Poets.*
>
> *Your impressions will be overturned again, swinging in the opposite direction; sometimes you will feel surrounded by strangers; other times by burning mirrors. Patience . . .*
>
> *Your voice murmurs: I will keep moving forward, trusting in my sensations, in my emotions, in the conflagration of my imagination, in my thirst to leave the land of shadows and silhouettes.*

Now the time of greatest value is coming, the time of the Creal-Poets.

When the old civilization has completed its fall, love will be there to guide us through the nights.

And, above all, the act of creating the world.

It seemed to us that the Great Destiny of the World was with us. But it depended on our desire, and on the fluidity of resistance. We surveyed cities, still too hard; we caressed the stones, and the palms of our hands vibrated. Those who thought us crazy, we decreed as dead. We were new-born.

Sometimes, one of us would speak of love as a gentle weapon. Another would respond: "Who loves well, punishes well." Other voices rose up, citing virtuous chance, magical conspiracy, friendship. There was much to relearn. While the realist sphere remained mired in the mud of definitions, we created a tabula rasa, *ready to redefine the soiled, meaningful words, one by one. Someone had said: "Obstacles are food for she who knows where she is going." Another added: "For one moving toward his own atmosphere, everything is oxygen. Deep in our hearts, we were joyful."*

We became lucid. Extra-lucid, even, at times, by refusing to adapt our vision to the accepted reality. We became able to see beyond form, our intuition awakening.

In great inhalations, our instinct returned, and wove a science of impressions, penetrating parallel universes.

Our limits are evolving. Yesterday's boundaries are not those of today. What defines the Creal-Poet is the invention of limits — the common construction, through oratory dialogue, of reference points that remain faithful to the sublime. An aesthetic of carriers, a spiral of joyous contagion. We are not strangers to one another, but loving accomplices in elevation. We fuse into armadas exploring the Living and the Unexplored. The torch of Being is passed from hand to hand, and without you I am nothing. We are explorers of dimensions.

In a bookstore in Oxford I found a copy of the *Bardo Thödol, The Tibetan Book of the Dead*. The book was intended, it seems, to free those who studied it from egocentric consciousness and its perpetual instability. It was read aloud to the dying, to guide them on the path to reincarnation.

It says that death itself is an illusion; it is only a passage. When I feel overwhelmed by my inability to understand the events that have turned my life upside down in the past few months, when I feel a bit frightened by the supernatural charisma and unreadable personality of my brother's son, I read a few sentences from the *Bardo Thödol*, and they calm me. Like this:

Noble son, with the body you have in this moment, you will meet your parents and friends as if in a dream.

A PARTIAL LIST OF SNUGGLY BOOKS

LÉON BLOY *The Tarantulas' Parlor and Other Unkind Tales*

FÉLICIEN CHAMPSAUR *The Latin Orgy*

BRENDAN CONNELL *Metrophilias*

QUENTIN S. CRISP *Blue on Blue*

QUENTIN S. CRISP *September*

LADY DILKE *The Outcast Spirit and Other Stories*

BERIT ELLINGSEN *Vessel and Solsvart*

RHYS HUGHES *Cloud Farming in Wales*

JUSTIN ISIS *Divorce Procedures for the Hairdressers of a Metallic and Inconstant Goddess*

VICTOR JOLY *The Unknown Collaborator and Other Legendary Tales*

JEAN LORRAIN *Masks in the Tapestry*

JEAN LORRAIN *Nightmares of an Ether-Drinker*

JEAN LORRAIN *The Soul-Drinker and Other Decadent Fantasies*

CATULLE MENDÈS *Bluebirds*

KRISTINE ONG MUSLIM *Butterfly Dream*

YARROW PAISLEY *Mendicant City*

DAVID RIX *A Suite in Four Windows*

FREDERICK ROLFE *An Ossuary of the North Lagoon and Other Stories*

JASON ROLFE *An Archive of Human Nonsense*

TOADHOUSE *Gone Fishing with Samy Rosenstock*

www.ingramcontent.com/pod-product-compliance
Lightning Source LLC
Chambersburg PA
CBHW032037180726
48284CB00008B/2623